TO HELL AND BACK

A DEVILISH DEBUTANTES NOVELLA

ANNABELLE ANDERS

CHAPTER 1

inally a Widow

"MA'AM. Please sit down. You've had quite a shock." The words barely registered as Eve Mossant processed that her husband of twenty years was dead.

Two years had passed since she'd last seen him. They hadn't lived together in over a decade.

She hadn't had relations with Jean Luc for thirteen years and seven months.

She was free.

"Mama." Her oldest daughter, Rhoda knelt beside her. Eve hadn't resisted when the gentleman delivering the news guided her to the sofa and lowered her to sit. "It's good riddance."

Eve nodded. "Yes." Yes, it is.

Her husband had been a libertine and a wastrel. Among other things.

She glanced up at Mr. Waverly, her man of business. He'd

handled her own fortune for the past year. Apparently, word had been sent to him first, rather than to the wife.

"How? When?" Did it really matter? It should. Perhaps if he shared some of the details she could believe the news to be true.

And although she'd spent years hating Jean Luc, tears welled in her eyes.

Mr. Waverly glanced over at Rhoda and her husband, Lord Carlisle, and they all nodded grimly.

"January twenty-ninth. Two days ago. Found dead in his bed. Smothered with his own pillow."

Eve processed the information stoically. It made sense. He'd likely angered some woman or her husband. Or perhaps been unable to pay one of his lady birds. And they'd held a pillow over his face.

The feat would have been easily accomplished as Jean Luc probably had passed out from drink or opium.

Or whatever potion he'd chosen to poison himself with that day. She wasn't sure what he'd most recently been dabbling in.

"Do they know who?" Again, it didn't matter. But a wife would be expected to ask.

Mr. Waverly addressed her question but, of course, the answer wouldn't matter. She stared out the window as two drivers skirmished over their vehicles on the street below. Ah, yes. One of the barouches had scratched the other. Unfortunate, really, it had been painted such a pretty color blue.

"Mama. Mama? Are you listening?"

Eve shook her head to stare into Rhoda's coffee-colored eyes. "But of course."

"I'll return tomorrow. After she's rested." Mr. Waverly's voice softened. His assistance had been indispensable to her. Since she'd come into her own fortune, he'd done his best to keep it out of Jean Luc's reach.

And he'd succeeded.

But before he could leave, Eve sprang off the sofa. "You are certain? This isn't some joke? Or a mistake?" Did she want it to be? Jean Luc Mossant had been her husband, after all. He was Rhoda, Coleus, and Holly's father — biologically anyhow.

Mr. Waverly stared at her solemnly. She'd not noticed how steady his gaze was. Had it always been so reassuring? So…solid? It must have been, for she'd trusted him with her lifetime security amounting to thousands of pounds.

And then he took both of her hands in his and squeezed. "I am certain."

"Did you travel to Pebble's Gate? Have you seen the body?"

"I did not. One of my associates brought me the news, and he is utterly reliable. But I will, if you'd like me to." He rose to his feet and moved across the room. He knew her circumstances well enough that he would comprehend her misgivings.

Eve took a deep breath. She hated losing her composure in front of anybody, particularly one of her daughters.

At least Coleus and Hollyhock were safely ensconced at Miss Primm's Ladies' Seminary this year. Since winning a considerable amount of money on a most disreputable bet, Eve now had the funds to pay the exorbitant tuition.

"I think the girls ought to be informed in person. Coleus will be most vexed to put off her coming out another year."

Not that Eve thought her husband deserved a full year of mourning from any of them, but society would judge them poorly if they failed to observe such a ritual.

"Rhododendron and I can go to the school, if you'd like," her son—in—law, a former vicar, suggested. Yes, her two younger daughters ought to hear of their father's death from Rhoda.

"Thank you, Carlisle." She nodded. "But don't pull them out of school. I don't want to compromise their educations right now."

"We'll come to Pebble's Gate afterwards, Mama." It was Rhoda who reached across to squeeze her mother's hand this time before glancing over her shoulder at her husband.

Lord Carlisle nodded in agreement.

3

Eve could not have been any more proud of Rhoda if she'd married the Prince Regent himself.

"And you will travel with her, Mr. Waverly?" Rhoda had turned to the sturdy man who'd done his best to disappear into the wallpaper. "I don't want her to go alone."

"I'll be fine," Eve interjected. She hadn't depended upon a man for years now. She'd learned the hard way that such laziness put a lady in some most disadvantageous circumstances.

"Of course. I'll make arrangements this afternoon, and we can depart early tomorrow morning. If that is satisfactory."

Eve wondered at the condition she would find the country property. At one time, it had been her home, but it had never belonged to her, of course. Jean Luc's nephew would inherit most of the estate. She wondered if the heir had been willed the debts as well.

God, she hoped so.

She needed to go.

Mr. Waverly could assist her with the funeral arrangements. And other legal matters, she supposed.

She pressed her fingertips against her forehead. "Tomorrow is fine."

As soon as Sixtus delivered the news of Jean Luc Mossant's death, Nigel Waverly had anticipated a visit to Bristol, the largest town near Pebble's Gate. She'd been a most unusual client from the beginning, and he quite preferred to handle the details of her business personally.

Not quite a year ago, he'd been asked to handle a rather delicate bet for Mrs. Mossant at the direction of Thomas Findlay. After she'd won, Findlay had sent him to her townhouse to discuss the management of those winnings. She'd proven even more interesting upon close inspection. His first thoughts were that she did not appear old enough to have three grown daughters. Elegant, slim, mocha-colored eyes, and shining chestnut hair, she could have been Lady Carlisle's older sister.

Ah, but there the similarities ended.

Mrs. Eve Mossant possessed a backbone unlike any he'd found in a woman before. Especially in a gently bred lady.

Developed out of necessity, no doubt. She protected her daughters like the lioness she had become due to enjoying absolutely no help from their father.

Eve had been decidedly pointed in what she required. She'd entrusted him with protecting her winnings from her husband at all cost. If Mossant had known his wife possessed such a fortune, he'd have wasted it away within a few months.

Nigel had no misgivings in doing as she asked. He'd heard of Mossant's libertine lifestyle.

During their first visit, she'd explained to Nigel, most unapologetically, that she needed the funds handled in a manner so that her husband would never have any legal right to them, which had been tricky, but nothing Waverly was not familiar with.

Nigel had then taken it upon himself to investigate Mr. Jean Luc Mossant. He'd even sent Sixtus down to Bristol from time to time.

Through those reports, he'd learned why Eve Mossant never allowed her daughters to dwell in the same residence with their father. And he'd respected her all the more for it.

A desire to safeguard the woman and her daughters had emerged in him. And as much as he hated to admit it, he'd been drawn to his client in a manner that had not been platonic. But although he remained a bachelor still at the advanced age of seven and forty, she'd been a married woman.

And a client.

First and foremost, he must remain professional. He'd never do anything to betray the trust she'd placed in him. His job was to protect her legal and financial circumstances.

She could purchase the townhouse she'd been leasing now, with no one else having legal claim to her possessions. He supposed they'd discuss much of this over the next several days. He'd have to go through Mossant's finances.

"Until tomorrow then, ma'am." He would leave her with her daughter and son-in-law for now. He had no obligation nor request to further his stay.

Nigel duly noted, however, that she had not collapsed at the news.

"Ah, yes, thank you Nigel." Her eyes appeared somewhat dazed. For her to have slipped and addressed him by his Christian name, she must be experiencing understandable distress.

He'd not offer his sympathies. In good conscience, he could not.

Nodding at the others in the room, he bowed and slipped out of the house. His carriage awaited. His office was situated within walking distance, but he hadn't wanted to delay the meeting any longer than necessary.

And now he had a journey to plan. He'd allow two days for travel in case of bad weather or difficulties. She'd ride in her own carriage, and he'd ride outside. All propriety would be observed.

CHAPTER 2

 anuary Rain

"Mr. Waverly has arrived, and the coach is ready outside."

Eve nodded toward her maid as she drew her favorite gloves on. They fit her perfectly, gliding over her hands to slide in place snugly like a second skin.

She would not make him wait. She knew other ladies made it a point to always be tardy, and that bothered her. It was disrespectful. And this was business. Her business, for which he was paid handsomely to attend to, and she needed to maintain a good relationship.

Jean Luc had been perpetually late. Even before his injury.

Eve glanced at Lucy but then turned again to study her more closely. Her skin seemed a little greener than normal, and she clutched her arms around her abdomen. "Are you not well, Lucy?"

The young woman sniffed. "Feeling queasy, I'm afraid." And then she pivoted and disappeared hastily into the dressing room.

Sounds of her maid's stomach discontent emerged all too clearly.

Eve frowned. This created something of a quandary. She hadn't considered traveling without a female companion.

Rhoda and Lord Carlisle would have already left for Miss Primm's.

She tapped her finger on her lips, contemplating her options, and then winced as more sounds of retching reached her ears.

They could delay travel — wait another day or two.

But Eve felt an urgency… She'd be quite uneasy, delaying in London, unable to look into her new situation.

She would travel today and have Lucy follow later. The luggage coach could be delayed until the maid was well enough to travel.

Decision made, she conveyed the new plans to her wan looking maid, retrieved her small valise, and made her way downstairs to meet Mr. Waverly.

Fifteen minutes late.

At her appearance, his brows rose. Of course, she'd never made him wait before.

"My maid has taken ill," she explained. "I'll be traveling without a companion."

His brows rose even further at this announcement.

"Very well." Of course, he'd not question her. He was in her employ, after all. "Might I suggest we postpone? The western sky is dark, and my assistant says his hands and knees are paining him. In the past, these two factors have always signified an approaching storm."

She did not want to wait.

"Is it raining now?" The weather had been too warm for snow.

"Not yet, Mrs. Mossant." His face remained impassive.

Eve did not want to be detained at home with so much awaiting her in Pebble's Gate. "I'd rather not delay our travel."

"Very well."

Mr. Waverly took up her small valise and held the door wide. A gust tore into the foyer and indeed, the air smelled like rain.

Outside, her carriage waited, along with the driver and one outrider. As well as Mr. Waverly's mount.

Of course, he'd not expected to ride inside the carriage with her.

Another gust lifted her hat, so that the string she'd attached it with tugged at her chin. The wind carried a few small droplets of rain.

Bleak clouds hovered in the sky along the direction in which they were to travel. Rain was indeed a certainty.

Poor Mr. Waverly wore a long coat and tall top hat. He'd be soaked in no time.

"You must ride inside the carriage until the rain passes," she suggested. If he wanted to do otherwise, that was his decision to make.

A few misgivings stirred her conscience when thunder rolled in the distance.

Again, his unassuming nod.

Eve climbed inside and settled herself comfortably. Within two minutes, he joined her.

She'd not expected his presence to be so overwhelming. However, within the tight confines of the carriage it was unavoidable.

He settled himself across from her, setting his hat beside him but not removing his greatcoat.

Eve had not looked at him so closely before. In her eyes, he'd represented security to her and his company had always been most reassuring.

But in close quarters, with no other distractions, her mind

trespassed on formerly untouchable ground. How had she not noticed his masculinity?

He must be over six feet tall. Although a few silver hairs grew at his temples, he still had a full head of hair. Firm chin. Broad shoulders, she knew, even without the extra material of his coat.

Jean Luc had lost most of his hair by their last meeting.

Jean Luc was dead.

She could still hardly believe it.

"He really is dead?" She asked the question without thought.

Dark gray eyes stared back at her solemnly. "I trust my associate to be accurate, but you'll see for yourself soon enough."

"He will have been laid out in one of the drawing rooms. If any of the servants remain. He wasn't ever one to inspire much loyalty." She tilted her head. "I hate to imagine the sort who will attend his funeral."

"Nothing for you to worry over, ma'am." Ah, yes. There was Mr. Waverly's reassuring response. "You won't be expected to attend. And according to my understanding, a butler and two footmen have remained. The housekeeper resigned last spring. Since then, the butler has been unable to retain respectable female help, as I'm sure you understand."

Another grumbling of thunder sounded, this one closer. Eve shivered and tugged her coat more tightly around her. They rode for some time in silence.

"I haven't visited in over two years. I hadn't thought to return so soon."

Mr. Waverly withheld his opinion on such a statement.

Eve closed her eyes and remembered that last visit. The man she'd married hadn't existed for years. She'd loved him once. So very long ago. Conflicting emotions threatened to overwhelm her.

"Jean Luc was thrown from his horse shortly after Hollyhock was born." She'd still been abed having suffered a difficult childbirth. "His physician assured me that he would survive, even walk again. What he failed to tell me was that my husband was consuming large quantities of Laudanum."

"Opium," Mr. Waverly supplied.

"Yes." Things had been difficult enough in that she'd only been able to provide him with daughters. "It managed to rob him of what little good character he'd had to begin with."

She hadn't spoken of this with anyone, although she suspected Rhoda had knowledge of most of it. "Initially, I assumed he was simply out of sorts, frustrated with his limp." Frustrated with me.

"And then I realized it was the tincture that changed him. He could not go a day without it. Without the medicine he became mean-spirited and violent." Eve shivered at the memory. "I hate the stuff. I'm certain it was sent to earth by the devil himself. If I'm ever injured or ill, I'd rather die than touch the poison."

Because it was poison. A very special poison that stole a person's soul.

She'd remained with Jean Luc until the day he'd nearly thrown Rhoda down a set of stairs. She'd been playing in one of the corridors with her dolls and had impeded his path.

"I'm sorry you had to go through that."

Eve swung her eyes back toward Mr. Waverly. "Thank you." Oh, but she'd been going on and on about herself. Likely he contemplated far more important matters.

"You never married, Mr. Waverly?" Before he could answer, an odd sense of envy struck her. Any wife of his would always feel safe and secure. She'd wager he'd be the most faithful, caring, and dedicated of husbands.

He would never threaten to kill his own offspring. Yes, such a woman would be lucky, indeed.

As he brushed his hand through that thick black hair of his, she noticed how elegant his fingers were. An interesting combination, efficiency and elegance.

"No, ma'am."

She ought not to probe. Normally, she would not even think

of it. And of course, it would be a shame to lose such an efficient and trusted man due to her prying.

"With all the traveling I did as a younger man, I didn't think it would be fair."

Indeed, if she'd been his wife, she'd not have been happy for him to go sailing around the world leaving her at home.

"You could not have taken her with you?"

A tight smile on his part.

Of all the conversations she'd had with him, they'd never discussed personal matters. Especially not his. And now for some reason his gaze stirred unnerving thoughts in her.

"I suppose." His eyes darkened. Or was that her imagination? "If I'd found the right woman."

And what type of woman would that have been? She dismissed the question before it could escape past her lips.

What on earth had come over her? He was her man of business. Even if her husband had not been a libertine, she was not the sort of lady who flirted.

Lightning flashed across Mr. Waverly's face. His nose looked as though it had been broken a time or two. Despite his present occupation, this man had obviously not spent the majority of his life sitting at a desk.

"Do you regret it?" Eve's daughters meant the world to her. Sometimes too much.

He shrugged. "Can one miss what one never had?" Another roar of thunder grumbled in the distance, and he leaned to peer out the window.

"I'm sorry." Remorse swept through her. "For insisting we travel. If you wish, we may turn back. I just…"

She had his full attention once again. "You just…?" he prompted.

"I just…" She had to search for reasons that she didn't fully understand herself. "I need to know it's over. I feel as though I've been running from him forever. He'd threaten sometimes, to demand the girls remain with him." She swallowed hard. "A part of me believes his death is too good to be true. And another part. There is another part that feels as though it's died." Oh, she wasn't making sense.

Dash it all, she would not shed tears for Jean Luc! She brushed at her eyes.

"I'm sorry. I'm being ridiculous." She sniffed. At the same time, a handkerchief appeared in her hands.

"No need to apologize. At one time you built your dreams around him."

"Which is ridiculous. It was so long ago."

She would not allow herself to remember what their marriage had been like before he'd changed. He'd presented her with an illusion.

But then a sob wracked her body. "I loved him once." She bent forward and buried her face in her hands. This was so embarrassing and yet she could do nothing to stop the waves of feelings rolling through her.

She had loved him once! A thousand years ago! She gasped on another sob. Of all the times to break down. Likely Mr. Waverly wished he were astride his mount, riding in the rain.

Mr. Waverly crossed to the bench beside her and then a warm and comforting arm dropped onto her shoulders. "Of course, you did."

Eve allowed him to pull her into the soothing warmth of his strength. Oh, to be held by another human being. To be the comforted instead of the comforter.

Jean Luc had lain to waste so many of her dreams.

"It was as though one day, he was a normal gentleman, a father and husband. And the next he was a stranger. And then something of a monster." Mr. Waverly's stoic demeanor methodically drew the nightmares out of her closet. She'd never spoken of this with anyone. He'd hold her confidence, of that she was certain. "I'm sorry to burden you with all of this."

"Hush." He reached his other arm up and held her tighter as the carriage rocked rhythmically.

So solid. So dependable. The wool of his coat felt rough against her skin. He smelled of leather and soap and that elusive scent some men carried: maleness.

"I spent a few years with the army. Would it help you to know that after a battle, a battle won, we not only mourned the loss of our own men, but those of our enemies? For each of them once represented a lifetime of potential. It is natural for you to mourn your husband. And I imagine you feel a good deal of relief."

She'd not realized he'd fought in any wars. His words gave her pause to wonder. The idea that one would mourn the death of one's enemy. It made sense. And all the lost potential of their marriage.

And so much relief.

Another sob took hold of her.

SHE WOULD BE MORTIFIED LATER, Niles presumed. That she'd allowed herself such an outburst in his company.

She must not have wept the night before. She would have busied herself preparing for the journey. He wondered if the woman had allowed herself to shed a single tear over the last decade.

He held her and shushed her occasional words of apology as the carriage rumbled away from the bustle of London. She'd grow calm for a few moments, only to be overcome again a few minutes later, with a fresh bout of sorrow.

Most men would feel all sorts of awkwardness to find themselves in such a situation. He, himself, might feel quite uncomfortable if it was any other woman. But this was Mrs. Mossant, and he felt an odd gratification that she trusted him to such an extent.

· · ·

HE'D NEVER EXPECTED to experience physical closeness with her. He'd imagined it, ah, yes, under quite different circumstances.

As her personal storm subsided, the gale outside did as well. Nigel made himself comfortable when he realized she'd fallen asleep. Emotional outbursts must be exhausting.

Feminine scents swarmed his senses. He focused on identifying them rather than the effect they had on his libido.

Lavender. Yes. And lemon. When he tilted his head forward, silken strands of hair tickled his chin and lips.

Careful not to awaken her, he turned both of them and raised one foot onto the upholstered bench, supporting them both with his other on the floor.

He would not sleep, but she seemed to need it.

Eve snuggled deeper against his chest.

Ah, yes, she would be quite mortified when she awoke.

CHAPTER 3

Mud

At first she thought she was sliding off of her bed. She gripped tightly to her pillow. Except this wasn't her pillow.

Much more solid than a pillow.

"Eve. Mrs. Mossant." Her pillow shifted and then gripped her arms tightly. "Oh, hell!"

And then the world tipped, shifted, and rolled. And rolled some more. Eve's eyes widened in time to remember she was not in her bed, but in the carriage. Her stomach lurched and her breath stalled in her lungs as the world turned into a chaotic nightmare.

Not the entire world, but her world, she corrected herself ironically as she watched her valise and then Mr. Waverly's hat bouncing off the ceiling of the carriage.

Crashing sounds, and the horses! Oh dear God, What of the driver?

She had nothing to grab hold of except for Mr. Waverly, who seemed to be doing his best to brace them from being tossed about any more than necessary.

By the time she was awake enough to gain her bearings, the carriage came to an abrupt halt. She vaguely heard the sound of horses running in the distance, and water trickling… Trickling right through the carriage.

"Mrs. Mossant?" The sound of Mr. Waverly's voice brought with it some reassurance. "Are you hurt?

Ah, her head rested on his chest. And they both seemed to be lying on the ceiling of the carriage. "I am unhurt, but what of you?" He'd taken the brunt of the impact.

She was afraid to move. What if they dangled over the side of a cliff? What if the carriage were to begin sliding again? Or rolling?

"I believe I shall live." Mr. Waverly moved gingerly. "Be careful, there's broken glass all around."

Pushing off of his solid chest, Eve did her best to free him without shuffling about too much.

"Umph."

"I'm sorry. Oh, dear." She'd planted her knee in a most unfortunate place. He groaned and then gripped her hips when she went to push herself off again.

"Hold on, woman. Not there."

Of all things. She was grateful for the semi-darkness so that he couldn't see the heat rising to her face. If she could only move her knee. "I'm— Mr. Waverly—"

Before she could finish, he'd efficiently released her from her skirts and moved her leg to one side.

Only now, she straddled him.

Her breath hitched. They lay on the brink of death and she was most certain that he'd become aroused.

17

Or perhaps it was merely his coat folded up awkwardly.

"Do you think we are in danger of falling farther?" She whispered the words, almost as though the sound of her voice, in and of itself, might send the carriage careening farther down the hill.

Mr. Waverly stretched his neck in order to examine their situation. As best he could, anyhow, what with her pinning him to the ceiling of this blasted contraption.

A tree branch protruded into the interior, the culprit that broke the window, no doubt, but the other was intact.

"I think we have quite safely landed at the bottom." His voice sounded tight. In that moment, she realized his hands remained upon her hips.

But moving was going to be a tricky endeavor, indeed, what with all the broken glass and what not.

"Don't move yet. If I can get my coat opened up, it might protect you from crawling on the glass."

"Oh, yes." And then, "You're bleeding." He must have hit his head in their fall. Dark red oozed onto his face from the top of his head.

"I'm fine." But he grimaced as though in pain, and for the first time since she'd known him, he sounded annoyed as he tugged his coat out from beneath him.

In doing so, the fabric of his pants met with the naked skin of her inner thigh. Somehow her skirts had tangled up in his coat. While purposefully avoiding his eyes, she struggled to ignore the very solid part of him protruding from behind his woolen pants.

"If you can climb over there..." He indicated the safe mound he'd arranged with his coat. "Perhaps I can open the door."

"Oh, yes." A solid idea indeed.

This time she moved with extreme care as she shifted her weight off him to kneel.

"Can you get up now?"

She stared intently at his hat, which had landed in the corner near one of her gloves. A tremor ran through her. "I hope the driver isn't hurt! And the horses!" This was all her fault. If only she hadn't insisted on leaving today.

"I believe he cut the tether when we started sliding." Mr. Waverly didn't sound overly concerned as he crawled toward the exit. Noises erupted outside. Shouts and scuffling.

"You two all right in there?" The driver tugged on the door at the same time Mr. Waverly gave it a solid push, sending them both tumbling into the mud.

Which drew a burst of laughter from Eve. Unconscionable of her to do so.

The two men scowled at her.

"I'm sorry." She covered her mouth. There was nothing remotely funny about their situation. She must be in shock. How was it that she'd contained her emotions so well for the past twenty or so odd years, and yet today she had unleashed a torrent of tears on poor Mr. Waverly and was now finding amusement at his expense? He was bleeding! They all could have been killed!

The terror of their accident was likely settling on her now, otherwise she would never have found merriment at the expense of others. The driver had landed on his bottom in the mud, and brown splatter dotted Mr. Waverly's face and coat. Her hands shook when she reached for her glove. She stifled another inappropriate giggle when she glanced back up.

Balanced on all fours in order to climb out, Mr. Waverly's backside jutted alarmingly close to her face. Before she could avert her gaze, she inadvertently noticed sinewy muscles stretching the gray woolen material of his pants.

Once the doorway cleared, he crouched outside and beckoned for her to follow. They must not be sitting on a cliff then.

Careful to avoid the shards of glass, she crawled across his coat to the door, peeked out, and met Mr. Waverly's gaze. "At least it's no longer raining."

"There is that," he responded grimly, and then he added, "No one is injured, but the horses have bolted."

"What should we do?" He'd have already developed a plan. He was an efficient, take charge sort of man.

He offered his hand and practically pulled her the rest of the way out the door. "Not sure how safe it is right here. More of the mud could come down at any moment. Best we find a way back up to the road." Wincing, he jerked his head towards a steep incline.

"Dear heavens? Did we come down that?" The sliding grooves and crushed greenery created by the carriage revealed how lucky they were to have emerged unscathed. She could barely see the top, where the road must be.

If it still existed.

"The climb isn't as steep over here." The driver was already scampering out of harm's way.

"My valise!" At least her trunks were on the luggage carriage, safely parked back in London. "And my hat."

She shouldn't bother herself with such trifles, but... a lady required certain accoutrements.

Pausing only the barest of seconds, Mr. Waverly dropped to his knees once again, and partially disappeared back into the carriage, allowing her another accidental glimpse of his fine—

"Anything else?" He'd backed up warily, in order to avoid the glass shards, no doubt. He'd retrieved her valise as well as her now crushed, velvet hat. He'd also recovered his great coat. Yes, that might come in handy at some point.

"No, that's everything." She took the handle of her small case and did her best to return her hat to its former shape before placing it upon her head.

Now. To find their way back to the road, the driver already having disappeared.

Standing, Mr. Waverly sent a somewhat puzzled glance in her direction. "Take my hand and have a care, the hill is slippery."

For an independent lady, she most certainly was relying a

great deal on her man of business. If only she could strike her early bout of weeping from his memory forever.

Warmth flooded her cheeks as he wrapped his fingers around hers.

"I'm sorry about earlier." She didn't wish to remind him of her weakness, but mortification forced the words past her lips. "I hope you'll accept my apology. It's not like me at all. I'm normally quite…"

"No need." He gave her a not so gentle tug. "We really shouldn't dawdle here."

"Of course." She managed a few steps before realizing something dreadful had happened. "Wait!"

What in the world? "The mud has eaten my slippers!" They were nowhere in sight. But they had been on her feet initially and she now stood in the mud, wearing only her stockings.

"It ate your slippers? Are you certain?"

"Mr. Waverly." She lifted one foot. "I'd hardly say so if I was not. Well, perhaps it didn't eat them, but it has consumed them."

For the very first time since becoming acquainted, Mr. Waverly seemed slightly amused by her.

She feigned annoyance with him.

She hoped this business relationship that had worked so well in the past endured this journey.

"Do you have anything serviceable in there?" He pointed toward her valise.

Oh, yes! "My half boots!" Except mud surrounded her completely and the stockings on her feet were soaked through and through. If she could manage to change into her other pair of stockings…

Mr. Waverly surprised her then, by dropping to one knee. What in the world?

"Sit on my leg, Mrs. Mossant. You can hardly lace up your boots while standing in the mud."

She paused only a moment. "That is very... gentlemanly of you. But would you mind closing your eyes?"

"Close my eyes? I do assure you that I've seen ladies' feet before."

"I intend on changing my stockings, if you don't mind."

"You—" He stopped himself. "Do hurry, though, we don't want—"

"I know, I know. We need to get out of here. But I can hardly walk with mud in my boots and I can hardly remove my stockings with you looking on."

A glimmer of a smile danced wickedly across his lips.

"Really, Mr. Waverly, I would imagine you might be more understanding."

She lowered herself gingerly onto the seat he'd created for her and reached beneath her skirts.

"These were one of my favorite pairs," she mumbled more to herself than to him.

CHAPTER 4

nd More Mud

NILES STEADIED Mrs. Mossant as she shifted and squirmed, her bum balanced precariously on his thigh. He tried not to imagine her hands skimming the length of her leg, touching feathery skin, in order to unfasten her garters.

Instead, he kept one hand at her back and the other ready to right them, lest her manipulations toppled them both over.

He dared not conceive the pain that might invoke. While tumbling down the hill, he must have slammed into something hard, bruising a rib.

Or two.

Or a perhaps all of them.

"There's one," she declared, taking his mind off the sharp pain in his left side. This time he allowed his mind to envision her sliding the hose down the length of her leg and off her foot. Sounds of the valise opening and her rummaging about kept him informed of her progress. Along with her nervous narrative.

"These are much more practical. Wool. My mother made them for me ages ago, and they've held up quite well. I brought them along so I could walk about the estate after we arrive. It's been a while, and I doubt Jean Luc has made time to visit any of his tenants."

And then, by her wiggling, he surmised she had her hand beneath her skirts again.

Focus on the mud beneath your knee, man. Even the pain in your ribs. Devise the next steps required to extract your client from this quagmire.

Yes. Client. Mrs. Eve Mossant was nothing more than a client.

He needed to get her up this hill and to the nearest inn as quickly as possible. Considering the damage the carriage had taken, he doubted it could be repaired easily, if at all.

Damn but he ought to have considered road conditions more than the desperate look in her eyes when deciding to travel in the wake of this morning's storm. He'd made a foolish decision and nearly gotten them all killed.

He inhaled deeply at his thoughts and winced. He didn't mind the inconvenience so much for himself, but he had a lady to protect.

Her hand landed on his shoulder, and she pushed herself off his leg. "There. Much better. You may open your eyes now."

She looked quite satisfied with herself.

He'd done well enough fighting his attraction to her in the past. He would continue to do so, regardless of her changed circumstances.

And he'd not find her straddling him again anytime soon. He'd gone without bedding a woman for far too long. He oughtn't to have been aroused. For God's sake, they'd just rolled down the side of a cliff.

"I think John went this way." He cleared his throat and gestured for her to walk in front of him. If she lost her footing, he could keep her from falling.

TO HELL AND BACK

Nothing untoward about the gesture. He'd do this for any client.

Squish. Squish. Squish.

Progress was painstaking and slow, but his respect for her only grew. If she had any complaints, she kept them to herself. And although she surely was experiencing a good deal of fatigue, she continued plodding right along. Until...

"Oh! Oh!" Both of her feet, planted on the ground, nonetheless, were sliding backwards. Her arms grasped at some nearby branches to no avail, sending her plowing into Niles' arms.

As luck would have it, he'd braced himself against a rather large boulder.

A soft bum pressed against him first, followed by rounded feminine curves. He caught her around the waist, just below her breasts, and tugged upward so that her feet didn't slither out from under her. He hissed in pain when her elbow jammed into his side.

"Oh, Mr. Waverly!" He'd expect a fit of vapors from most ladies of his acquaintance but was to be surprised by her once again.

She was shaking with laughter.

Bent over, unable to breathe, uncontrollable laughter.

"I'm sorry." She barely managed the words. "It's just that..." More laughter. "Why had I thought this would be easy? Anything having to do with my husband was never simple."

Her dead husband.

A carriage accident.

And yet a few unchecked chuckles escaped his throat. She could barely hold herself upright and tears had begun streaming down her face.

"Oh, don't laugh. I'll never be able to stop." Her laughter went unchecked for a full minute before she was able to successfully bring it under control. By then she had turned around in his arms and was wiping at her eyes, leaving some rather pronounced muddy streaks in the process.

He didn't think to stop himself from grinning at her.

Hanging onto his shoulders, she suddenly stilled. "What?" A wide smile filled her face. "I've not gone mad. I promise you. Despite." She used one hand to indicate her dress, her shoes and her face. "I imagine I can either laugh or cry. And as you well know, I've already given in to the latter..."

Niles couldn't help but study her animated face.

So full of life. This woman.

"I much prefer this," he allowed himself. He'd been happy to comfort her but hated that she was experiencing such turmoil. Yes. He'd always prefer laughter.

He swallowed hard, suddenly uncomfortable at such intimacy. Her face, tilted up, and her hands clutching him, left a scant few inches between their lips.

When was the last time he'd kissed a woman? Not out of lust, nor convenience, but because he wanted to?

Since curtailing his work for Findlay a few years back, he'd lived an almost celibate existence. While traveling... not so much.

But he'd avoided romantic entanglements.

"Hello there! Mr. Waverly." A shout from above had Mrs. Mossant dropping her arms and turning around. "I'd like to go after the horses, if you don't mind?" John was obviously becoming impatient waiting for them.

Niles turned various scenarios around in his brain before answering. "Meet us at The Goat and Pig. Mrs. Mossant and I will make our way there on foot!" Unless another respectable vehicle came along.

And if it could remain on the muddied road.

He'd traveled this route before. The Goat and Pig didn't offer luxurious accommodations per se, but it would provide a safe haven for his client until other arrangements could be made for her travel. He took a deep breath and immediately regretted it.

Blast and damn this mud.

"We've passed the midway point, I believe." This to encourage her. "Try to step on the larger rocks. You're less likely to slide that way."

Without looking back again, she straightened her shoulders and took a few tentative steps in the direction she'd just slid down. This time, he grasped her waist from behind. Somewhere along the climb, they'd lost her valise. He hoped she hadn't been carrying anything valuable. He supposed he could send someone back for it, if necessary

The going was slower now, as the top half of the climb dropped steeper than below, but they made steady progress.

Her feet slid a few more times, and her knees buckled once, but she kept moving without complaint. By the time they arrived at the road again, her face was flushed. Beneath her silly hat, damp tendrils of hair clung to her forehead and the sides of her face.

She swept the hat off her head and glanced between the two of them. "That was quite stimulating." Illuminated by sunlight, for the first time, he noticed a few strands of silver hidden in her coiffure. Tiny lines crinkled at the corners of her eyes as she stared off into the valley below.

And then the glow of the sun disappeared, and with it the silver glints and harsh illumination.

A dark and threatening looking cloud moved visibly across the sky.

"I don't trust this road. Are you able to continue toward the inn?" Although no longer as vigorous as he'd been as a younger man, he had retained his stamina by practicing the ancient arts.

She would be quite fatigued by now, despite the satisfaction she'd derived from their climb.

She grimaced. "I'm sorry, again, for all this." She turned to walk, but in the wrong direction.

"Do you plan on hiking back to London, then?" His words halted her.

"Oh. Of course not."

Niles gestured for her to go ahead of him, but then reconsidered and took hold of her arm. "This way to The Goat and Pig."

"They'll take one look at us and surmise the establishment was named for the two of us."

Niles chuckled.

A woman who maintained her sense of humor under such circumstances was rare indeed.

WHAT A DISASTER of a predicament this was!

Eve matched her steps to Mr. Waverly's. She wasn't a petite woman, but even so, she surmised he'd shortened his stride so that she wouldn't struggle to maintain their pace.

"How far is this Goat and Pig establishment?" she dared to ask. Perhaps they ought to have marched toward London. If they were lucky, some passersby might come along and take them up. She'd abandoned her belongings when changing her footwear, leaving her with nothing respectable or even clean to change into.

All she had was her traveling dress, a light wrap she'd donned earlier that day, and her hat — and even that was ruined.

Mr. Waverly squinted into the distance. "I'd hazard to say five miles? Difficult to say as it's been a while."

Five miles? She stifled a groan.

What would she tell her daughters if they were in her situation? To be grateful they'd come out of the mishap uninjured? To dwell on something other than the crick in her side or the blister on her left heel.

Chin up, Eve.

"Does your work require you travel often, then? Your other clients?" She'd keep her mind preoccupied by learning something about her dedicated man of business.

"Not as much as in the past, but oftentimes Findlay has me look in on the factories. Most of those are up north." She, herself, had met Niles through Thomas Findlay, father to Rhoda's friend, Cecily. The man's success in commerce was quite legendary.

"How did you meet Mr. Findlay?"

"He gave me my first job." This might prove interesting after all. She knew very little about employment of the merchant class.

"As his secretary?"

Niles chuckled and then winced. "I suppose my duties fell more under the title of... security."

Fascinating.

"You were one of his brutes? A ruffian?" Common knowledge provided that Mr. Findlay did not achieve all of his objectives by following established practices. She turned her head so that she might study Niles Waverly more closely.

"For a few years."

This would explain the less than perfect line of his nose. And his very solid presence. Even tumbling down a cliff, she hadn't experienced fear.

He'd protected her with his own body. She hadn't considered it at the time, but that was why she'd been entangled with his person when they'd landed.

"What did you do after that?" He'd piqued her curiosity for certain.

His jaw clenched, and she wondered if he resented her prying.

"I became something of a manager."

"You managed all the other brutes?"

"Among other things."

"Is that why you never married, then? Because you were constantly putting yourself in danger?"

He shrugged. "I suppose. And the travel."

Walking side by side with him, she couldn't help herself but to study Mr. Waverly again. "Did you grow up in London?"

He slid her a sideways glance. "I did."

She wanted to know more. Had he been very poor? Who were his family?

"And you, Mrs. Mossant, where do you hale from?"

"I grew up on a small country estate, not far from Pebble's Gate."

CHAPTER 5

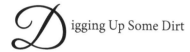
igging Up Some Dirt

HE COULD IMAGINE HER UPBRINGING. Protected. Entitled. The daughter of landed gentry, betrothed at a young age to the son of a neighboring land owner. He'd known enough of them.

"I grew up in Mayfair," he provided.

Not sure why he'd tell her this. Perhaps because she seemed to want to know. He'd set the record straight. Allow her an understanding of how he came to be the person he was today.

A man with genteel manners, but grossly below her, notwithstanding.

"My father lived in a gardener's hut, set behind the Earl of Peabody's London manor. My mother worked in the Earl's kitchen. His lordship was kind enough to keep her on despite their improprieties."

"You grew up in Mayfair?" Clearly, he had indeed surprised her with this information. "I'm well acquainted with Lady Ester, his youngest daughter." Her brows furrowed then.

It ought to come as no surprise to her. He'd grown up a servant to her equals.

Although employed professionally now, in essence, he still considered himself something of a servant on occasion.

He'd believed himself in love with Lady Ester's older sister at one time. Ah, yes, he'd been a foolish lad back then. And he'd learned his lesson well.

Lines between the classes were as immovable as oceans and rivers. Perhaps more so.

"My father was a baron," she chimed in. "Spoiled me rotten as a girl. My mother had probably been spoiled worse than me." She scuffled along, her head down now. "Never in my life have I found an unhappier woman."

He could think of no suitable response, so he offered none.

After a fashion, she continued. "She hated my father. Found fault in everything he did and everything he said. Can't imagine my father was all that happy either. Tell me, were your parents in love?"

"Ridiculously so," he answered without thought. His parents had spent almost every waking hour working but when they did manage to find time together... "Embarrassingly so," he corrected.

They continued talking in this vein for the next several minutes. Surprisingly, they'd both received similar educations, his out of charity, and hers as had been expected.

He respected her, but more surprisingly, damnit, but he liked her. He found himself sexually attracted to her even more so than before. Of course, he'd never act on it. Or so he'd convinced himself.

She stumbled, causing him to halt and assist her in finding her balance. She was exhausted. He ought to have paid more attention. It wasn't the distance that required so much effort, rather the clawing mud and the terrain.

"We can stop for a while." A large tree that had fallen alongside the road caught his eye. "Sit down." Likely she was parched, as well. All this mud and not a drop of fresh water between the two of them.

"Are your parents still alive?" She brushed at the log before finding a seat upon it.

Niles lowered himself gingerly beside her, stifling a groan at the pain that shot through him.

"The earl has provided them with a small pension and a cottage to make their home on his country estate. His lordship is a decent fellow." Something Niles himself had brokered. With a certain degree of arm twisting.

She'd referred to her father in the past tense. "What of yours?"

"My father passed a few years after I married. With no son to inherit, my childhood home went to a distant cousin, whom my mother married. She still resides at Neptune's Park, but her health is diminished."

Niles wondered that he'd not learned this about her earlier. "And the cousin?"

A tight smile. "Ironically, not dissimilar from Jean Luc." And then she shook her head slightly. "I do not visit often."

Damn. The masculine half of the population had not given this woman much reason to trust their sex. It was no wonder she'd sought her independence so diligently.

She tipped her head back, closed her eyes, and inhaled. "It's going to rain again." She spoke the words quite matter of factly.

She was right. Clouds had been gathering in front of them for ten minutes now.

She slid a glance at him from beneath her lashes. "Under normal circumstances, I appreciate the scent it brings."

"But not when one is caught unprotected in the elements," he agreed, doing his best to ignore the surge of attraction he experienced — ignore his imagination...

33

They ought to be on their way again, but he'd not push her.

He needn't have worried. She rose and offered her hand. "Shall we then?"

To assist him.

With him being nearly twice her weight.

They barely walked ten steps before the wind kicked up, carrying with it a smattering of sprinkles.

"I'm so sorry for this. I should have considered the road conditions more seriously." This was his fault. She'd insisted they travel, yes, but he could have refused her.

She ducked her head as the sprinkles turned into pelting drops. They couldn't proceed in such conditions. He grasped her hand and tugged her towards a copse of trees in the distance. At least they'd afford a modicum of protection.

Again, her fortitude surprised him.

A bolt of lightning flashed with its thunder not far behind.

EVE HADN'T RUN in ages. As in moved faster than a walking pace, lifting both feet off the ground at one time.

Holding this man's hand, exhausted and quite undone, memories from her youth tantalized her. Of climbing trees and playing in the rain.

She might feel differently if it was colder, but for now, she felt renewed somehow.

When they reached the trees she wondered at who she'd become, but then scoffed at herself. The death of Jean Luc had scrambled her in more ways than one.

Oh, but this storm was magnificent. Warm hands grasped her from behind and vigorously rubbed the length of her arms.

"Oh, Niles. May I call you Niles? I forget how powerful nature can be!"

His motions slowed and for a moment, she felt his chin

resting atop her head, as though he too would take a moment to appreciate the spectacle. "You're a unique woman."

"Eve," she supplied. "Call me Eve." Under such primitive circumstances, it felt odd to address one another by either Mister or Missus.

"Eve." His voice sounded husky. From their exertions, likely.

"I am different than most of my counterparts anyways." She knew she wasn't like other ladies of her acquaintance. Ladies who'd lived their entire lives dependent upon husbands, brothers, and fathers. Her daughters, she knew, would be different as well. It was why she'd sent the younger girls to finishing school this past year. She wanted them strong, but without the sharp edges she herself had formed.

Although she did admit, such strength had saved her eldest. She shivered and his arms wound around her middle. She covered them with her own and leaned against his solid warmth. Mr. Waverly — Niles — was different too.

In all their dealings, he'd never acted controlling or overbearing. Yes, she employed him. But other business managers had tried manipulating her. Other business managers she'd utilized had gone to her husband to question her decisions.

Niles had not.

"You're different in a good way," he supplied.

The words warmed her even more than his body. She'd lived amongst the ton for most of her life but oftentimes felt like an imposter. Less feminine. Less respectable.

Just.

Less.

"Thank you."

Perhaps she could drop her defenses with him because he was not one of them. Despite his demeanor and speech, he had never been a member of the upper class.

His manners and dress were impeccable. And, yes, his looks

quite surpassed those of most younger men, let alone men his own age.

But he was not another nob seeking any means available to pay off his debts. Abhorrent as the notion was, she'd been protected by her marriage. Now a widow, in possession of considerable funds, she'd best be wary.

But not with Niles.

Her very own Mr. Waverly.

And then she caught herself. What on earth was she thinking? He wasn't her Niles. Her Mr. Waverly. He was her man of business!

She stepped out of his warming embrace, wrapped her own arms around her front, and shivered again as a gust of wind swept through her.

Her gown was soaked, through and through. Even worse, the storm showed no signs of letting up. In fact, the sky looked even darker in the distance.

They'd found themselves in such dire straits due to her self-ishness and impatience. As she berated herself, she was vaguely aware of Niles moving around behind her. He'd said nothing when she'd pushed herself away from him. Was he feeling the same fleeting, completely temporary attraction that she had?

There was, of course, the moment directly following the crash, when she'd felt him—

"Come sit down. It's dryer back here." How was it that he could speak such an edict without it sounding like either a command or an invitation? He was speaking to her in his man of business voice again.

She turned to find that he'd fashioned the bulk of his great coat into a small tent of sorts.

Eve could be stubborn or she could be warm.

Another shiver.

"Thank you."

Making her way farther into the brush, she found the ground

less soaked. The branches overhead were thicker, more tangled with each other. She dropped to her knees and then edged into the small shelter.

It would be cozier if he were sitting beside her. They could share one another's warmth.

He remained standing, however, a few yards away from the shelter he'd built. He would not attempt to join her, she knew.

A flash of lightning and then more thunder.

Niles cursed. She didn't think she'd heard him curse before. So contained. Throughout their acquaintance, until today that was, he'd always held himself removed, respectfully aloof, professional.

Was that why she'd not noticed him, as a man before?

Well, of course she'd known he was a man, but was that why she'd not noticed the solid width of his chest, the chiseled line of his jaw? The sensuality in his smoky gaze?

Not that any of it made any difference.

Her fingers fluttered to her chest. Try as she might, she most certainly was noticing him now.

"Niles."

He paced away from her, toward the clearing.

"Niles." She said his name louder this time. "Won't you please come out of the rain? You're no good to me if you fall ill."

He glanced over his shoulder, meeting her eyes. "Damnit, but I ought to have insisted we delay travel. I ought to have considered—"

"Niles," she cajoled with a gentle smile. "If it's anyone's fault, it's mine. Please, won't you come and warm up? Then I will argue with you over who gets to take the blame for this debacle."

He jammed his hands into his pockets and then reluctantly turned and did as she asked.

He was careful, she noted, to touch her as little as possible. As soon as he settled, she edged herself closer to him.

Strictly for warmth.

He stiffened at first, but then dropped an arm around her shoulder and relaxed slightly. She'd made matters awkward by pulling away from him earlier.

One question swarmed through her mind as she soaked up his heat.

What should she do now?

CHAPTER 6

𝒮trictly for Warmth

NILES BERATED himself twice over for allowing this situation to deteriorate to its present conditions. The temperature had dropped, and their damp clothing clung to their bodies.

Furthermore, he could not deny he'd made her uncomfortable by talking to her, and touching her, in an overly familiar manner. Calling her Eve, even at her request, complicated the boundaries of what had been a circumspect relationship.

She'd revealed a great deal of herself to him today. He wouldn't read anything into it. He'd simply been there when she needed to cry, and later as they hiked, to pass the time.

"I refuse to allow you to blame yourself for all of this." She broke the silence between the two of them. "I absolutely demand my half of it, Niles, if not sixty percent."

She was calling him Niles again.

"I thought the inn was closer," he admitted. "And if you insist, I'll allow you thirty-five percent, but no more than that."

She chuckled and nuzzled closer.

He would not take advantage of their physical proximity. She must feel vulnerable, lost. As much as he'd like to run his hands along the length of her body, to steal a taste of her lips, he wouldn't.

Even if she was now an unmarried woman.

Who, this very moment, trailed her fingers down the front of his shirt in the most intoxicating manner.

On a hiss, he reached up to stop her. "Mrs. Mossant."

"Eve," she corrected him.

"Eve..." But he did not push her hand away. Instead, he raised it to his lips. "You are not quite yourself today."

"Perhaps you are right." She sighed loudly. "Or perhaps I am more myself than I have been in a very long time."

Holding her fingers against his mouth, he allowed himself to drop a single kiss there.

He'd not realized that he'd missed tenderness. Unwilling to break the connection between the two of them, Niles closed his eyes and...let his senses take over.

Instead of pushing them away.

For a moment. He'd allow himself this moment.

She moved her hand to explore his face; her fingers danced across his eyebrows and then her hand caressed his jaw and the skin along his ear. When she dropped her hand abruptly, he exhaled. Had he been holding his breath?

"I'm proving to be a nuisance, aren't I, Niles? First, I weep on you for over an hour, then I nearly topple you down the hill, and now I'm making matters even more awkward. I'm sorry if I've made you feel uncomfortable. You are right. I am not quite myself." Even though her words registered, her body said more. She maintained her position in close concert with is body.

"You are not making me uncomfortable." God help him. His own inclinations did quite well on their own. Just sitting beside her, sharing their warmth, tempted him.

"You don't have to say that. I'll allow I've relied on you inappropriately for most of this journey." Her voice sounded throaty, most unlike the Mrs. Mossant he'd come to know in London. "You're likely wishing me to perdition." Her hand rested on his chest.

She was making this impossible for him.

"You are my employer, a woman all too recently widowed. It would be unfair, unethical of me..." He stared straight ahead and surveyed the clouds. The storm had picked up strength along with their own barrage of emotions.

"Oh, Niles. If you only knew."

He shifted both of them so that he could see into her eyes. If they were to have this conversation, he'd look at her while doing so.

"If I only knew what?" He pressed.

She took a deep breath, as though for courage before answering. "How badly I need you to be unethical today."

Steady, sultry eyes met his with unabashed need. Her cheeks were flushed and those lips of hers parted slightly.

Dammit.

He could resist his own need, but not hers.

She would require comfort now. She'd lost a husband, a horrible one at that, but a husband, nonetheless.

He needed to be certain. Niles leaned forward and paused. "If you wish."

But she backed away an inch. "Don't feel that you have to. I only thought—mmphh"

He cut off her speech demonstrating the requested absence of ethics.

At first her lips felt cool, cold even, pinched tight. How long, he wondered, since she'd been kissed?

"Open for me," he mumbled against her. "Relax."

She nodded, slipping away until he could capture her mouth again.

This time her lips parted softly beneath his. He lifted his hands to cup her cheeks, and then the back of her neck. Her tongue retreated at first but grew bolder to eventually dance and tangle with his as the kiss lengthened.

Oh, but he loved the essence of a woman, this woman. Her deliciously moist mouth tasted sweet, earthy, her teeth glided smoothly against his tongue.

A tremble flowed through her, whether from the cold or the kiss, he couldn't be sure.

"Hold me," she whispered.

He drew her closer, dropping his arms around her shoulders and then her waist.

How long the kiss went on, he wasn't sure. It could have been a minute, or ten, or more even. He lost himself as he took inventory of her responses. A hitch, a moan, a gasp.

The way she spoke his name, half whisper, half groan.

Eventually he became aware of a quieting. The thunder had drifted away, and rain no longer pounded everything around them.

And their private tempest settled as well.

Niles placed one last kiss on now familiar lips and drew in a heavy breath. They were two consenting adults. But he would not take her on the ground, on the dirt.

If, and that was a very big if, he were to take her at all, it would be on a comfortable bed dressed in clean linens.

He tucked her head beneath his chin and waited while she steadied her own breathing.

"Your name fits you rather well."

"Hmmm," she mumbled into his shirt front.

"You tempt me, Eve. Now tell me, was that unethical enough for you?"

EVE STRUGGLED to comprehend his words.

So long. She'd waited so long for something so simple as a kiss. There had been days when she'd surmised, she'd live the remainder of her life untouched.

He'd reignited sensations she'd feared might be dead — Niles had — her man of business.

He'd asked her something. Was that unethical enough for you?

She managed to nod, her face pressed against his chest now.

"Thank you," she whispered into his waistcoat.

"The storm's passed. I'm afraid we must set out again. The mud will be worse than before, but we need to make the inn before darkness falls." His voice sounded rather matter of fact. Obviously, the kiss had affected him far less than her.

His arms dropped away, and she stiffened. What was she doing? What had come over her? Most assuredly any kiss would have sent her thoughts into such a jumble. "Yes. Yes, of course." She wished she could have risen to her feet gracefully.

But no. Not only was her dress jumbled around her legs, but pins and needles plagued her left foot.

Holding his side, Niles rose easily.

"Are you injured?" Had she done something to him, or had he injured himself earlier?

"It's nothing." He offered a hand to assist her up.

She rearranged her skirt and wiggled her toes before taking it. Once standing, she studied his eyes. "You would not be holding your side if it were nothing. You foolish man! Why didn't you say something?"

A small injury could become serious all too quickly. Unfortunately, there was nothing to be done until they arrived at the inn. Or any shelter, for that matter.

Without answering her question, he offered an arm and led them back toward the road.

"I don't mean to call you a foolish man. I do that to my daughters, you know." She couldn't help explaining to him. "When they worry me."

"You call your daughters foolish men?" He would make a joke of it. Who was she to worry about him?

"Foolish girls." She ignored his teasing.

Mentioning her girls reminded her who she was. A mother. A mature woman, not some starry-eyed miss. That kiss back there... It meant nothing. A bit of comfort. Warmth. She was the foolish one, to have imagined for a minute that it might lead to anything else.

But now you are a widow.

Eve ignored the taunting voice in her mind.

And you haven't been kissed in over a decade!

She pushed her shoulders back and stared into the distance.

The road was, indeed, more sludge than anything else. She'd thoroughly ruined her boots by now and doubted Lucy could repair her dress which was now frayed and muddied at the hem. Hopefully the traveling coach would pass through tomorrow.

Neither she nor Mr. Waverly spoke another word for what felt like hours, making slow but steady progress. And then, just when she couldn't stand another second of his silence, a sign came into view.

Aged and worn, nonetheless, it directed them off the road toward The Pig and Goat Inn. Not too promising, but shelter. Water. Safety.

Greater relief than she'd imagined, swept through her. They would not be forced to spend the night in the outdoors after all. Each time they'd rounded a corner and come upon more open road, her worry had increased. Although doing his best to hide it, Niles was obviously in pain. She didn't know what she'd do if he worsened.

She glanced at him in time to catch an expression of relief crossing his features, as well.

"I shall certainly sleep better than I did last night." She broke the silence. Exhaustion would ensure the rest her body craved. She'd lain awake the night before thinking of Jean Luc. But now, after tumbling down the side of a mountain, his death didn't seem quite the traumatic event that it had initially.

Was traumatic the proper word for his death? His life had been traumatic. Their marriage had been disappointing. His death was...

Final.

That's what it was. Final. No more need to fear him. She'd stopped hoping he'd changed ages ago. But he was the father of her daughters and now he was dead.

They made their way around some brush, and the inn appeared by the side of the road. Simple, unadorned, nothing special about it at all, but it might as well have been heaven. Niles held the door wide so that she could precede him inside, and a few minutes later, he was handing her a key.

"Room number three. He's sending his wife up in a few minutes with dry clothes for you to change into." He spoke impassively, back to being Mr. Waverly. Disappointment bothered her.

Surely, he hadn't forgotten? And exactly how pathetic was it that she'd thought of practically nothing else. Could she blame it on the rain? Shock from having her carriage go tumbling into a ravine?

"Thank you." She wrapped her arms around her front. "About earlier—"

"Forgotten." He shoved both hands into his pockets, answering her unspoken question.

Yes. Yes. That would be best, would it not? Put it behind them, as though the kiss never occurred?

"Has John been here?"

Niles grimaced. "Not yet. I imagine if the horses took off in another direction, they might have headed back toward London. But the innkeeper says they have a gig we can rent. I'd prefer we allow the mud to dry, however, before continuing on."

"Of course." She glanced at the key in her hand. "What room are you in? That is, in case I have need of you." Being with him and counting on him like no other made her feel like a young girl. Much as she'd first been with Jean Luc before…

With her man of business of all things!

"I'll be in the tap room." Again, his face impassive. His demeanor cool. Did he intentionally not want her to know which room he would be sleeping in? Or—

"You didn't hire a room for yourself?"

"All full up, Mrs. Mossant."

"Oh, don't 'Mrs. Mossant' me." Were all men this foolish? "And with you being hurt!"

"Eve—"

"Come with me. You need to rest. Did you think I didn't realize your ribs have been paining you? Did you tell them who you were? Did you give them both of our names?"

"Just my own."

"Well, then. They'll have to imagine I am your wife or some such nonsense. You need a place to sleep and I need to not feel guilty for your injury. It's not as though I'm some innocent intent upon protecting my virtue." Eve would not sleep a wink knowing Niles was trying to sleep on a wooden bench for the night.

"I'll find a cot."

"Nonsense." She grasped him by the arm and pushed him in the direction of the stairway.

He was surprisingly compliant. The pain must have worn him down more than he'd let on.

"Eve—" He made one last attempt to argue but seemed short of breath.

"Hush."

CHAPTER 7

*S*haring

As much as this new turn of events bothered him, Niles ceased resisting her after she'd removed his coat and then coaxed him onto the bed. His entire body ached. Not just his chest or his side. Every blasted breath he took pained him.

Damn ribs.

He watched from half closed lids as she put a candle atop a dresser and then one beside the bed. Thank God they'd arrived when they did. Night was falling.

He should get up and leave now.

She was his employer. He had no business in here.

A knock sounded at the door. Must be the innkeep's wife with something for Eve to change into. He closed his eyes and drifted off to the sounds of Eve chatting with the woman.

When he next awoke, he required a moment to remember is whereabouts.

Ruined carriage. Mud. Rain.

Kiss.

This time when he watched her, the candlelight glowed warm upon her skin. She was sitting on a hard chair, staring off into the darkness as though deep in thought. She ought to be the one in bed. She ought to be the one resting comfortably, sleeping.

In their normal course of business, he'd easily managed to suppress his attraction to her, but after today...

And now seeing her in nothing but a too-large cotton night rail with her shining chestnut hair flowing over her shoulders and across her softly rounded breasts... her desirability further strained his self-control.

Such a woman would not be a burden, as a younger lady might. No, Eve Mossant would present other challenges. The sort of challenges that made a man want to wake up each morning.

Because, oddly enough, she exuded strength. She inspired confidence.

He closed his eyes again, shutting her out. He'd not allow his thoughts to travel in such a direction. He'd done that once before, with a lady, no less.

Lord Peabody's daughter, Lady Katherine.

Niles would do well to remind himself of the dreams he'd built around her. He'd been all of twenty-one, and she'd just turned eighteen. She'd come to London for her debut. Throughout the years prior, they'd been friends. As children.

But she'd been different that spring, as had he. And she spent hours in the garden, confiding her disdain for the young bucks of the ton to Niles. None of them had inspired her love. They were too weak, too silly. She'd flirted outrageously with him, touching his arm, glancing at him from beneath those lush lashes of hers. He'd held out for less than two weeks before succumbing against his better judgement.

Ah, but the excitement of a secret love affair.

They'd done nothing more than share a few amorous embraces, but those had been enough to inspire love on his part.

He'd begun dreaming of a life with the earl's daughter. They would run off together. He'd find a way to provide for her, and eventually a family.

By the end of the season, he'd formulated quite the plan.

And then she'd told him she had become engaged to a young viscount. She was to be married in the summer.

Niles had thought she was joking. It seemed impossible that she could live her life without him.

Even now, he disparaged himself for his naivete.

He'd not make such a mistake again.

He needed to absent himself from Eve's room. Already, that kiss…

It caused his heart to ache along with all the other aching muscles plaguing him.

"Niles?" She spoke softly. He opened his eyes to see her studying him, holding a cup of something. He'd not heard her cross the room to kneel on the floor beside the bed. "Can you drink? I wondered if you might want to eat something. I had some bread and cheese delivered earlier. And some whiskey. And willow bark powder. You need something to ease your pain."

"Eve." The word sounded hoarse. He ought to be taking care of her. "How long have I been asleep?" His body screamed at the idea of sitting up.

"Just a few hours." She touched his forehead with her fingertips. "You've a fever."

She looked like an angel, kneeling there, dressed head to toe in white. Niles managed to lift his hand enough to touch the curling ends of her hair. He'd wanted to touch her hair for a long time now.

Silky and soft. What would it feel like on his face? On his chest?

"Drink this." She was bending over him now, holding the cup to his lips. The scent of lemon and something floral surrounded him with feminine comfort.

He didn't want to disappoint her and so forced himself to sit up enough to swallow most of the liquid. The willow bark left a bitterness on his lips.

And the sitting had sent shards of pain knifing through his chest and side. When he inhaled sharply, his reward was another stab of pain.

Hell and damnation. "Whiskey?" If he could down a half a bottle, that might relieve some of it.

She offered him a spoonful.

At least he wasn't required to sit up again.

"I believe you might have broken one of your ribs."

Or two, or three... "I have. Not the first time. Nothing to be done." If he remembered correctly, the injury had required nearly a month to heal.

"Rest then." She spoke firmly. "And you'll need out of those clothes."

At some time, she must have removed his boots. Damn, he'd have made a mess of the bed linens with the mud on his trousers.

Efficient hands were unbuttoning his waistcoat. "Get these off and I'll give you more whiskey," she murmured, apparently sensing his reluctance.

Oh, agony and some twisted delight on his part. He'd not bargained on the feel of her hands skimming his bare skin while she managed to tug his shirt over his head

"It is bruised and swollen here." Careful fingertips grazed the now exposed area along his side. "And here." She touched the spot just below his left breast. "Let's remove your trousers, Mr. Waverly."

"Damnit, woman." Niles was not used to such helplessness. "I can manage."

"It's not as though I've never seen—"

"Eve," he warned. This was not the way he'd imagined getting naked with this woman.

Smirking a little, she turned around.

Niles fumbled with his falls and kicked them off his legs. She barely gave him time to slip beneath the woolen blanket before turning around. Not that he was modest but, God dammit, she was his blasted employer!

He dropped back against the pillow, his breathing shallow.

Fine man of business he was turning out to be.

EVE WORRIED at her bottom lip. How had the man hiked all that distance with such an injury? She doubted he would have said anything if she hadn't asked. He'd have slept in his damp clothing, most likely on a wooden bench, hoping to leave her none the wiser.

Men!

When she'd explained to the innkeeper's wife that her... husband... had injured himself, the woman had offered her some tincture with opium. Eve had flatly refused. She'd not be any part of ruining her Mr. Waverly.

She was willing, however, to spoon whiskey down his gullet. He'd gone pale after disrobing, and she hated how shallow his breathing sounded.

She'd dribbled nearly half the bottle of whiskey into his mouth and enjoyed a few warming sips herself.

When had she last been alone with a naked man? She laughed at herself and took another swallow of the spicy liquid.

Feeling unusually bold, she trailed her hand from the base of his throat nearly to his navel.

She remembered that her husband had worn padding to simulate the physique that was all too real on this man.

There was nothing false about Niles Waverly's masculinity. Was her mouth watering? Oh, for heaven's sake, Eve!

Pale skin stretched taut across his chest. Even at rest, the skin on his arms hid sinewy chords, as did his abdomen.

She reluctantly drew back her hand and studied the stubble

appearing on his chin and jaw. Dark circles etched beneath his eyes, but the rest of his face flushed with fever.

"I'm going to call for a physician." She wobbled slightly as she rose to her feet.

"No, Eve." Niles grasped hold of her arm and slanted a hooded glance in her direction. Drunken or pain ridden, she wasn't sure which. "I've injured my ribs before. Nothing they can do. Now–Lie–down–Bissside–me... You–sleep–too..." His normally eloquent speech quite deteriorated.

There was not much room left on the small bed, but it appealed a great deal more comfortable than the floor.

He tugged at her with surprising strength, considering his condition.

"The candles," she chastised him.

His hand relaxed, and Eve left his side to snuff them out.

No one would ever know that she'd slept in the same bed as her man of business. And really, the floor would be quite uncomfortable. Likely Niles himself would forget if she awoke early enough.

She took one last swallow of whiskey for courage before lowering herself onto the surprisingly soft mattress. Odd, that she found the mattress to be soft. Inn bedding usually left a great deal to be desired. Perhaps it was just that her body was so very, very tired.

She tucked a hand beneath her chin, and turned onto her side, careful not to make contact with the large but injured man on the bed beside her.

"Are you awake?" Being alone didn't normally bother her. She'd been alone, but for her children, most of her life.

"Hrgmm," Niles mumbled in answer.

Now that she was lying down, her mind came wide awake. With Rhoda married and the girls at school, she'd been alone but not...widowed.

"I won't cry on you. I promise. I just. It's just that." She struggled to express what she was feeling. "I absolutely hated Jean Luc in the end. He was a horrid person, as you well know. But apparently I sat alone with myself too long this evening. Too much time for thinking. But now, having done so, I cannot help but feel as though something is missing in my life." By this point, Eve figured she was mostly talking to herself.

What was missing in her life?

Her identity?

"It's almost as though I'm no longer a whole person. The girls are growing up, Rhoda's married. I no longer have my mother, really, or the home I grew up in. Jean Luc's cousin will eagerly take ownership of Pebble's Gate to take ownership." She hadn't acted as the mistress there for years, nor would she again. It was all so final.

She stared at the side of Niles' head, just as though he was listening raptly to her every word.

"I'm no longer a wife, and yet I have a great deal of my life left to live. At least, I hope I do. But as who? Who am I now?" The question taunted her even as she spoke it into the quiet night.

"Eve Mossant." Apparently, he'd not dozed off.

"What?"

"You asked who you are. You're Eve Mossant."

And then he surprised her by turning his head and meeting her eyes. "Only now, you are free to be whoever you wish to be." He gazed at her with stern but hazy eyes. As though chastising her for questioning her own strength.

"It's silly, I know. To be afraid." The man was going to believe her completely daft by the time they arrived at their destination. He probably already did.

But instead of looking annoyed by her, he reached one arm up and pulled her closer to him. "You're not silly, Eve. And your fear is only natural."

Why were tears welling behind her closed eyelids now? She'd just promised him that she would not cry again.

It was the sympathy. And the comfort. She was not used to it, especially from a man.

"There were times when I wished I'd never married. But then I wouldn't have had Rhoda or Coleus or Holly." Her daughters brought her so much joy.

"You're a good mother, Eve. Not many women would have found the means to protect their daughters as you have."

His words brought her some comfort. But she'd only done what was necessary.

"What of you? Do you ever wish you'd married? Had a family?" She didn't want to talk about herself any longer. But she was only met with his deep, even breathing.

Eve relaxed into the side of Niles' very solid form. She could not remember ever falling asleep in her husband's arms. She might have been a great deal lonelier over the past decade if she had.

The heat of his body mixed with hers. The bedcovers cocooned them in a sanctuary she had not known existed. She felt safe, protected, connected.

And she rather liked it.

$\mathcal{M}$orning

IN THE NORMAL course of his days, Niles didn't require a great deal of sleep. Usually he performed most efficiently with less than five hours, and often did so on four.

Today, however, would not be one of them.

Although a bright light filtered through the curtains, and he had details to attend to in order to organize the remainder of their journey, he made no effort to move.

His ribs hurt worse now than they had yesterday.

Furthermore, a warm, pliant woman was curled up beside him.

Eve. He barely remembered the confessions she'd shared before he'd fallen asleep. Anger stirred in him at the thought that this woman was feeling lost.

She mumbled a few unintelligible words and buried her face against his shoulder. Her hair tickled his chin and her sweet scent wafted into his nostrils.

A woman such as her deserved so much more than she'd been handed in marriage.

Her slim leg slid along his.

Her feet tangled in his. She'd awakened, obviously, but...

Doubts assailed him. He oughtn't feel so uncertain at his age. This woman assaulted his senses and created havoc in his normally astute brain.

And then her hand slid up his chest.

He was not yet ready to return to being Mrs. Mossant and Mr. Waverly. Hell, he didn't think he ever would be.

"I've proven quite the nuisance of a client, haven't I?" He wondered if she laughed half-heartedly at her question or her actions.

Client be damned. He'd put an end to this here and now. He could not think of her as a client this morning. He doubted he'd ever relegate her to such a position again.

Pain hounded his left side, she warmed his right. Ignoring the stabbing sensation of moving, he rolled in her direction.

"Enough."

"You would deny that I'm annoying?" A teasing smile lifted her lips.

He chuckled softly and studied her in the morning light.

He could hold her more easily like this. Skim his free hand along the length of her in order to divine feminine curves beneath the large gown. Dips and flares. He buried his face in her hair. "You aren't a client this morning."

"Niles." She buried her fingers in his hair. "We shouldn't."

Ah, but he would.

This kiss differed from the one they'd shared yesterday. Earthier. Heartfelt and yet, raw.

Different than any kiss he could remember. Was it the woman herself, or was it him?

She'd joined him in the bed — in only a night dress. He could touch her freely. They would not be interrupted.

She arched her back, pressing into him.

"Eve."

She opened her eyes and stared back at him. He needed to know she wanted this before going any farther.

One tear crept out the side of her eye. She blinked it away and nodded.

"I want it. You can't imagine..." And then she closed her eyes and pressed closer.

Realistically, he couldn't satisfy both of them this morning. Hell, he'd barely been able to turn onto his side.

But this.

This he could do.

His hand wandered downward again, over the soft mound of her abdomen. He watched her lips part on a gasp. God, he loved the pale skin of her neck and shoulders. Bending to trace her pulse with his lips, he discovered skin that tasted as delightful as it looked.

Gathering her gown in his fist, inching it upward so that he could touch the bare skin of her leg, seemed the most natural thing in the world.

He pushed the gown aside and traveled his palm over the soft skin of her thigh. And then up and around to cup a warm, heavy breast.

"Niles." She clutched at him almost frantically as he settled his hand between her legs. A little pressure here, and then inside. Slick and warm. Niles dipped his head to her breast and nuzzled her above the material of her gown.

She trembled and squirmed, trying to get closer as her gasps came quicker. "Niles." She spoke his name in awe. "I can't. I'm not. I don't know what—"

"It's all right, love. Let go. Open for me. Ah, yes." He encouraged her release. "Just like that. Beautiful, oh, my beautiful Eve." His voice broke on her name.

She was Eve.

"Niles, please, please," she begged. "Oh! Oh!"

He pulled away to watch her lovely face as she found her satisfaction. Ecstasy, pain, delight, and then gratification. The crimson flush of passion only enhanced her classic beauty.

No tears now. Just a soft, sensual, lazy smile.

His own arousal persisted, but he disregarded it. This had been about her. His gaze memorized her curves, the dips and shadows of her belly and the dark curling hair entangled with his fingers. When she let out a sigh, he removed his hand and reluctantly eased her gown down to cover her again.

"I'm afraid to open my eyes." Her voice sounded sleepy. "I'm afraid this is just a dream. I'm also afraid it's all too real."

Her honesty gave him pause.

He could not read more into this than there was. Eve Mossant had been born into the upper classes. He was all too aware of society's constraints. God damn him if he fell in love again.

He turned onto his back and stared at the ceiling.

"Nothing more than a moment in time, Eve. We must seize life's pleasures when offered." Did he sound as stilted to her as he did to himself?

And then she rose on one arm and was leaning over him. Brandy colored eyes met his. "Niles. Thank you. Thank you for offering me one of life's pleasures. I haven't..." She shrugged almost imperceptibly.

And then her lips found his.

And like her smile, this kiss unfolded lazy and slow. They savored it like a decadent dessert after a gourmet meal.

When she drew back, he couldn't help but ask, "How long?" The question was inappropriate, he knew, but all of this was inappropriate. And he wanted to know more of her, her secrets, her desires, her dreams.

She winced. "Too long."

"You never sought intimacy outside of your marriage?" Would

she answer him? He half expected the question to send her into a rage.

"I did not." She looked as though she might apologize. But then, "What of you? Have you had somebody special in your life? Someone to warm your bed at night?" She flushed pink at the second part of her question.

EVE TRACED HER FINGER ALONG NILES' shoulder.

None of this made for appropriate conversation. They'd gone well beyond being appropriate with one another.

Niles had never married. A part of her hated imagining him alone, lonely, but another part of her hated even more, the idea that a woman awaited him somewhere.

"On and off," he answered vaguely.

Niles touched her face and then lifted his chin to demand another kiss. Oh, how lovely to touch another human being like this again. To be kissed. To feel another person's hands on her body.

During the early months of her marriage, Jean Luc had kissed her, but he'd not seemed overly comfortable doing so.

Those kisses had never made her feel like this — like she could melt into him. Not that she could remember.

It had been so very long.

"Did you never come close to marrying? Did you never fall in love?" She had no idea as to the etiquette required after such an intimate act. Could one ask a lover about previous… lovers?

He captured her lips a second time. More melting. Exploring.

"Are you avoiding the question, Mr. Waverly?" she half teased him when their lips parted on a sigh.

"No. Just couldn't help myself, Mrs. Mossant." And then he shifted himself so that she lay half on top of him. "I was in love once. Hard not to ever experience the ailment over the course of four decades."

"What happened?"

"She didn't feel the same."

"And you haven't been in love since? Was she the love of your life, then?"

"I don't have to tell you how painful it is to be disappointed after you've handed over your heart. After you've trusted some-body." He sounded so serious. And yes, he was correct.

"I'm sorry she hurt you."

"It was a long time ago."

She would not press him. Love had the power to imprint wounds one would rather forget.

She knew that this — whatever it was between the two of them — was not love. It could not be. She pushed herself to a sitting position and shivered as cool air met her upper half. "I'm not sure what to do now. I'm quite naïve about matters such as these, Niles." She avoided meeting his gaze, instead focusing on the privacy screen. She'd done her best to clean the gown she'd been wearing yesterday. It would be presentable, she supposed, glancing wryly at her boots.

"Matters such as what, Eve?" She felt his gaze uncomfortably.

Rising and then moving across the room, she shrugged. "Moments of pleasure?" What did one call this sort of thing?

"What would you wish?" By now, he was sitting up, looking perfectly at ease with the conversation.

"I... I don't know," she mumbled, stepping behind the screen and out of his sight.

"How about we start with breakfast?" Laughter rumbled in his voice. Part of her wanted to admonish him for joking about her uncertainty, but the relief washing over her drowned that part out.

"And tea," she added, pouring water into the basin. This was normal. She knew how to conduct herself well enough, performing normal tasks. "Are you able to come downstairs?" His color seemed better today. "I can have something sent up if you'd prefer to lie abed."

He didn't answer so she peeked around the screen, catching a glimpse of him fastening his breeches. Standing, fully clothed, he appeared once again to be the business man she'd come to rely upon.

Only now she knew the texture of his skin. And she remembered how hard his body had felt pressed up against hers.

When he glanced up, he seemed to be suppressing a grin. As though he could read her mind. She lifted her hand to tuck some stray hairs behind her ear. He didn't force the issue, however. "I'll meet you downstairs in half an hour. I'm going to see what I can do to acquire some sort of conveyance for us to travel in tomorrow."

Tomorrow.

Pebble's Gate.

For some reason her heart dropped at his words. He sounded anxious that they be on their way. She ought to feel the same. Hadn't it been she who had insisted upon traveling without delay?

"Yes. But of course."

"Eve." He turned back and captured her gaze. Something in his eyes flared, sending an unexpected warmth swimming through her. "Moment by moment."

He'd apparently realized her uncertainty. She nodded, feeling foolish but also comforted.

"I'll meet you downstairs then." What would they do for all of a day in one another's company? They certainly could not remain in the chamber!

CHAPTER 9

*I*nterlude

THE LIST of details he'd subconsciously catalogued regarding Eve Mossant was becoming amazingly long.

She drank tea with one spoonful of sugar but no milk. She brushed her hair behind her ear whenever she was nervous. She mumbled in her sleep.

And after being intimate with a man, with him, she turned up shy.

Niles had especially enjoyed the blush that crept up her neck when he stared at her with a certain knowing. As though she too, was reliving the intimacy from earlier that morning.

He'd reserved a gig for the two of them to rent the next morning. It wouldn't be as luxurious as the coach they'd lost, but he deemed travel would be safe.

Leaving the two of them with today...

He'd told her it was important to seize the moments of pleasure life offered and then decided to take his own advice. Leaning back in his chair, he studied her.

She all but glowed.

Ah, yes, he'd embrace whatever pleasure life presented in the now.

They had shared a comfortable late morning meal. She'd initially picked at her food, quietly, until he'd asked after her daughters' schooling. Afterwards, they ventured outside for a short walk, but returned quickly, unwilling to wade through the mud again.

Eve was polite to everyone they met, and during a short conversation with the innkeeper's wife, discovered the existence of a very small library set off from the tap room. This provided a few hours of amusement for them. Both favored several authors in common and despite the pain Niles experienced with each breath, what ought to have been a banal afternoon, proved to be rather enjoyable.

This woman.

Her company had made yesterday quite tolerable as well.

"Can the bishop jump other pieces?" Eve's question drew his attention back to the board they'd discovered set up near the window. She'd confessed to not having played in years. She could not remember all the rules, she'd admitted. A game was exactly what they needed. He wasn't certain either of them was ready to return to the chamber he'd rented.

"Only the knight can jump." He patiently explained, watching her fingers turn the piece so she could study it. Although it was not an expensive looking set, someone had put a great deal of care into carving the wooden pieces.

Once play began, she caught on rather quickly. Already, she was establishing her pawns in the center of the board.

"It's difficult to plan one's moves far in advance." She scrunched her nose up, deep in concentration. "And contemplate every possible scenario." She frowned and then slowly slid her bishop across the board making it so that she could utilize her queen.

Which was exactly what he'd failed to do the entire course of this journey. Examine every possible scenario. Plan his moves in the unlikely event that he might find himself sharing a bed with her.

"Emotions cloud your strategy," she added.

Indeed, they did. He could escort her back to their chamber. And then what? Turn his back while she donned that ridiculously large night dress? Feign sleep when she climbed into the bed with him?

Or would he make love to her, in truth, tonight?

Could his ribs survive it?

And what if she took offense at his advances? He'd lose this tenuous but pleasing connection they'd established with one another. And yes, he could lose a valuable client, but even worse, she'd be without protection.

She slid a pawn sideways and took his rook.

Damn, but he'd lost his concentration.

Four moves later, he'd placed her in checkmate. He'd not insult her by allowing her to win.

She was disappointed but immediately went to lining the pieces up for another game. "You're a devious man, Niles Waverly." She laughed and moved one of her pawns forward two spaces. "I'd always thought the game represented war, but it's more than that, I think."

"It's often used to practice military strategies." But it was so much more, he agreed to himself. Niles matched her next move. "Anything that involves strategy," he added.

"For example?"

"Business dealings." He briefly explained one scenario he'd orchestrated for Mr. Findlay. An opening bid. A counter. Negotiations and eventually capitulation.

She listened carefully as they took turns opening up the board.

She frowned and nodded. "I recognize similarities in how I evaded my husband throughout the years. He'd make a move and I would counter. In the beginning, I acted defensively. Toward the end, I made my own moves. I set up my own strategy to protect the girls from his influence, from him." She bit her lip. Almost as though she'd revealed more than she'd intended.

He'd change the subject for her. He knew well enough of Jean Luc Mossant's treachery. "Miranda plays chess with Ferdinand, in the Tempest. It's the only time the Bard ever referred to the actual game of chess, as far as I know. Although he used the terms of chess numerous times." Niles eyed the board thoughtfully. "Checkmate. Stalemate. All the strategies of chess could be found in his work."

He grinned as she took one of his pawns and then fluttered her eyelashes at him. "Sweet lord, you play me false." Eve, of course, knew the scene he referred to.

Niles searched his memory for Ferdinand's response... "Not for all the world." He could not recite the line word for word. Miranda had accused Ferdinand of cheating so that she could win. The entire plot had been something of a chess match.

"In the middle ages, it was one of the only activities where a couple could spend time together, alone. Even now..." Eve frowned at the pieces before her.

Niles moved his piece into position.

He'd been allowed to play chess with Lady Katherine. What harm was there? He had been the gardener's son. She'd gotten angry with him when he'd put her in check mate. She'd told him it wasn't gentlemanly to play to win.

Niles had countered by reminding her that he was not, and never would be, a gentleman. Lord, but that fact had come back to haunt him.

He'd never played the game with any other woman. The

subsequent women he'd spent leisure time with would not have been interested in such entertainment.

Until today.

"Chess can also resemble a courtship." A mysterious smile played on Eve's lips. Her flirtation was having a dangerous effect on his libido. And his heart. Because he knew their dalliance was not a true courtship. He'd do well by himself to call it a fling. An affair. A temporary liaison.

"An opening bid." He moved a pawn. What had his bid been with her? Holding her in the carriage? Kissing her beneath the trees? Or bringing her to satisfaction in bed this morning?

Her gaze teased him as she moved her queen across the board. "A counter." She'd kissed him back, eagerly. And she'd admitted to not knowing how to conduct herself following such intimacy.

Did she want something more?

He moved his knight in position to take the lady. "Negotiation." Was their time today a negotiation of sorts?

Could they have anything other than a brief affair?

She stole the knight with her bishop. Best not to want more from her. Had he learned nothing from Lady Katherine's betrayal?

Niles then moved his other knight. "Checkmate."

EVE HAD NOT SEEN his attack coming. She'd thought she'd examined the board from all angles.

Niles cocked one eyebrow, appearing quite roguish. This day, rather than bringing any clarity to their situation, scrambled them all the more.

She liked him.

The attraction she felt had only managed to increase as the day slipped away. His eyes shone brighter, his smile held more charm... Each time they drew near to one another, the urge to lean into him, to feel his strength along the length of her body, was quite compelling.

Would she resist him for long?

"I remember why I gave the game up now," she said, laughing.

"You played quite well."

"A rematch in the future, then." She didn't catch herself before allowing the words to escape.

"I'd like that very much," Niles responded noncommittally. Would he really, or was he simply being kind? She was his employer, after all, she reminded herself for the hundredth time that day.

"You don't have to."

But he'd reached across the board to take her hand in his. "Eve. This." He waved his other hand between the two of them. "Is not business."

No. It was not.

The day had passed almost without her notice. She'd been so intent upon this man. On the sensations he evoked each time he touched her, whether he'd taken her arm, or placed his hand upon the small of her back.

"I'll leave you to celebrate your win while I dress for dinner." The innkeeper's wife had managed to locate something clean for Eve to change into. The dress, of course, wasn't nearly as fine as any of Eve's other gowns, but it was freshly washed and the right size.

She'd like to appear her best for him.

Niles squeezed her hand. The look on his face held promises for the evening, perhaps for the night, ahead.

"I'll be counting the minutes."

CHAPTER 10

 omance

AFTER WATCHING her disappear up the stairway, Niles lowered himself onto a bench in the taproom and ordered a strong drink. Whiskey. A newspaper's headlines caught his attention as it lay on the table before him.

A ship had sunk off the southern coast last month. The Estonia. He'd have read more but could barely see straight for the discomfort each breath caused him. Niles had not invested in its cargo. The temptation had been strong, but he'd had a feeling... A few of his associates had thrown their money down. Poor fellows.

He ordered a second shot. A double this time.

Right now, she was dressing for him. Just a few short days ago, the thought would have been unimaginable.

She'd not contradicted his statement that what was happening between the two of them had nothing to do with business.

She's been flirting with me.

The evening ahead stretched into what ought to promise an abundance of pleasure.

He'd spent the entire afternoon in her presence, and already anticipated her return. He suspected she felt the same. Surely, he was not mistaken.

The tension had been building between them all day. They would draw it out even further, over their meal.

And after.

He would take his time with her. Undressing her slowly, revealing her skin inch by inch. And then he would taste all of her before settling himself between her legs.

Damn. This could only lead to trouble.

He groaned, turned sideways, stretched out along the bench, and closed his eyes.

Breathing proved less painful in this position.

"NILES." He opened his eyes to a concerned looking Eve staring down at him. "Why didn't you say something? You're in pain, aren't you? I feel horrible, keeping you out and about all day."

Had he really fallen asleep?

He refused to endure any more pity from her. Not with this one night left alone for the two of them. "I'm fine. Just resting my eyes." Ignoring the stabbing sensations, he rose and bowed over her hand. "For which you're a vision this evening."

She eyed him suspiciously, but also blushed at his compliment. "You are certain?"

He laughed. Niles had endured far greater pain in his life. He'd been much younger, of course, and he couldn't quite remember when exactly, but he must have experienced worse at some point.

He winged an elbow and led her to the most private table in the room, set near the fireplace, too small for more than two people.

She'd pinned her hair up, but not too severe. A few curling tendrils fell softly around her face.

And her gown, although simply made, enhanced her subtle beauty. She'd always looked beautiful to him. In the past, her gaze had been friendly enough, but she'd kept herself reserved.

Tonight, her eyes glowed with a sensual light. As though she too savored the promise of what lay ahead.

"I'm famished," she announced as he held her chair.

"Getting thrashed at the game of chess tends to do that to a person." He enjoyed teasing her. She hadn't been teased nearly enough.

"Oh you!" She waved a napkin at him. "Distracting me at every turn."

"Wasn't I," he contradicted, "who provided the greatest distraction."

The meal passed in a blur of flirtation and seductive glances. When he would think back on it later, he would have no memory as to what had been served.

He'd remember the lady and the wine. The latter of which he'd managed to slip a few swigs of whiskey in between.

He'd remember the anticipation building.

The sensations invoked as their inhibitions disappeared.

She spoke of some of the dreams she'd had as a girl. She'd wanted security. Children.

A kind husband.

She hadn't expected a loving husband or a handsome husband. Her only requirement had been that he be kind.

In turn, Niles told her of the land he'd always wanted to purchase along the southern coast. He owned it now and had commissioned the construction of a practical home.

"Oh, but how wonderful for you!" She'd not been impressed, it seemed, so much as happy for him. "When will you live there? You aren't going to retire anytime soon, are you?"

In fact, he already had. He responded noncommittally, remembering to whom he was speaking.

But then she'd announced that he simply must take her there to inspect it. Her and her girls, she'd corrected.

Most of his dreams, he realized in that moment, had come true. He'd stopped dreaming extravagantly the day Lady Katherine announced her betrothal to her viscount.

Eve asked about the landscaping, the furnishings, and deigned to make a few suggestions. He could almost imagine her making his house into a home.

Both their tongues had been considerably loosened. Every empty silence filled with expectancy.

By the time they climbed the stairs to their chamber, the energy in the air sparked between them.

"Goodnight Mrs. Waverly ma'am, sir." The innkeeper's wife nodded at them in the corridor. They'd easily passed themselves off as husband and wife. Niles didn't remember stating such a falsehood, perhaps Eve had.

He liked that about her. That she was willing to do what she had to for the greater good.

He held the door wide and watched her walk into their chamber. She wasn't acting coy. She hadn't asked him to wait downstairs while she prepared for the night.

Ah, no. Tonight would be theirs.

He just may have consumed enough spirits to quiet the pain in his ribs. He could do this.

He would do this.

With his back to her, he locked the door and allowed himself a tight wince before quickly replacing it with emotions he'd rather have her see. Appreciation. Desire. Lust.

All of which coursed through him at an alarming rate.

She stood in the middle of the room, arms wrapped around her front. She appeared shy and uncertain now that they were alone again.

He'd not give her a chance to shut him out. "God, you look beautiful."

"Are you certain?" Hesitancy laced her voice, but anticipation lit her gaze. "I'm not unaware that you're in pain today."

In three long strides, he held her in his arms. "Does this seem uncertain to you?" He'd have liked to scoop her up and carry her to the bed, but even with the greatest resolve, he didn't think it possible. Instead, he walked her backwards until they both fell onto the mattress.

Oh, hell. An unwise move on his part to be certain. He covered his shallow breaths with a few chuckles.

Because she was laughing now.

Laughing and lying beneath him.

Careful to keep most of his weight off her, he reached one hand to untie his cravat. "Are you certain?" He would have her assurance. "You've suffered a loss." At her raised brows, he conceded "Not a great one, but a loss nonetheless."

Slim arms wound around his neck, pulling him downward.

Pain.

But this was Eve, and he'd make love to her... this once.

"I've wanted to do this for so long." He confessed the words against her lips. Perhaps he ought to have kept the sentiments to himself, but—

"Don't wait any longer," she commanded, equally breathless. Her hands finished untying the sloppy knot he'd tied earlier and then worked his shirt out of his breeches and over his head.

An amazingly efficient woman. Damned if he would complain.

While his ribs protested, he turned his mind to her mouth, her breasts, her thighs... In a frenzy, they undressed one another with a familiarity as though they'd been doing it for years.

Except their passion was new. Burning and fresh.

As was the stabbing pain in his side and chest.

Niles had managed somehow to remove all her clothing

before dropping his face into the curve of her neck. "Eve." He could not have imagined the combination of nervousness and anticipation he'd feel with her.

And a level of trepidation. He wasn't exactly at his best this evening.

But this was Eve.

When he lifted himself to hover over her again, something thick seemed to lodge itself in his throat. The trust behind her gaze slayed him.

She was not a young girl in her twenties. She was a woman. A mother. She'd been a longsuffering wife.

And yet she could somehow trust him.

"I'm so glad it's you." She murmured the words as his mouth covered the pulse at her throat. "Niles."

"Eve." All he could manage was her name. And yet, it was everything. She was everything. Giver of life. Temptress. Her namesake had led to the fall of man. Would she lead to his own demise? He wondered vaguely that his heart might be obliterated completely by the time this, whatever it was, ran its course.

He didn't care.

He pressed against her core. So wet for him. Legs wrapped around his thighs, ready to pull him closer.

If only each breath he managed to take didn't make him feel as though his chest was about to crack open.

His ribs would heal eventually. He focused on the sensations where they joined and continued moving rhythmically.

Damnit. The pain was becoming impossible to ignore.

Eve's hands clutched at his back as she arched upward. He needed to keep going. Just a few more minutes. He was close, so close, as was she.

He hated that he might be missing any of this.

And then...

She was trembling in his arms and pulsing around him. He exercised all the patience he could muster and then withdrew in one jerking motion, found his own release, and then collapsed into a heap of satisfaction and agony.

"Niles."

He couldn't quite answer her. Hell, he could barely breathe.

"Niles?" Concern filled her voice this time, and he could feel her leaning over to peer at him. For the second time in as many days, he lay helpless and pathetic, at this woman's mercy.

"Ribs," he finally managed. He'd not want her thinking he was about to expire.

DAMN FOOL-HEADED MAN had scared her half to death. Brought her to the height of passion and then collapsed lifeless beside her. She ought not have allowed him...

Well.

They shouldn't have...

Only.

The evening truly could not have ended any other way. And he'd insisted he was well. The thought that he'd been willing to make love to her despite the pain in his ribs was somewhat flattering.

The day had been a most memorable one. She'd never forget it.

So instead of drowning herself in recriminations and regrets, she cleaned herself up and then located the willow bark powder for Niles.

And after assisting him to down all of it, climbed back into bed beside him and enjoyed sleeping beside a man.

It might be the last time she ever had the opportunity.

CHAPTER 11

*H*arsh Morning Light

"MRS. MOSSANT!"

A woman called out above sharp knocking, no, pounding coming from the other side of the door. Her voice sounded quite similar to that of her maid's, Lucy's.

Eve bolted upright. "Lucy?"

Oh dear. And here she was in bed with her esteemed man of business.

With Niles.

"Aye, Mrs. Mossant! I've one of your trunks out here. John explained what happened with the other carriage. You poor missus! If you unlock the door, I'll bring your belongings inside and have you set to rights for traveling today."

Niles had jumped out of bed and was already pulling his breeches up. Eve located his boots and shoved them into his arms. "Hide while I distract her."

She could not have Lucy finding her in bed with Niles. Her maid was known for her lack of discretion.

"Just a moment!" Eve stalled while Niles shoved his feet into the well-worn boots and stepped into a hiding spot behind the door.

John, the driver would be downstairs. As would be the outriders.

Eve opened the door and drew Lucy inside toward the privacy screen easily enough. From the corner of her eyes, she caught sight of Niles slipping out behind them.

Thank God!

"I was beside myself when John showed up in town yesterday! Without you and Mr. Waverly. You could have been killed! Or worse! Oh, Missus, that night rail isn't fit for you to wear at all. You poor thing. John's changing out the horses and said he'd be ready to leave for Pebble's Gate as soon as you are."

Eve's head was swimming. With a glance outside, she realized the sun was halfway up the sky. She and Niles had slept away most of the morning.

Lucy rifled through the trunk she'd dragged as she continued her rant. "Innkeepers downstairs are crazy as they come. Said you'd checked in as Mrs. Waverly. John's looking for that man of business of yours. Likely he's making some deal or another..."

Niles would smooth matters over, she had no doubt. He was very good at that. It was probably why Thomas Findlay had found him to be so useful.

They would depart for Pebble's Gate again. Soon.

Was it over? This tryst between Niles and herself?

Eve lifted her hands in the air so Lucy could assist her in changing. Perhaps her own clothing would help her feel more herself again. What would her maid think if she knew what had occurred in that bed last night?

"We mustn't forget to return the gown to Mrs. Pinkerton."

The innkeeper's wife didn't seem to be a lady of many possessions. She'd been kind to share what she had.

Lucy added dried lavender to the large washing bowl and poured fresh water into it. A wash cloth. Laundered chemise and stockings. Clean shoes.

Eve's gaze settled upon the unmade bed. Thank Heavens her daughters would never know what she'd done.

She shuddered at the thought and then waves of shame began washing over her.

Niles must think her a wanton. If he'd respected her before, he certainly couldn't now.

She'd acted no better than a common––

"This gown is ruined." Lucy studied the frock Eve had hiked across half of England in. "Shall I leave it here? One of the maids will appreciate it."

She'd intentionally donned one of her uglier gowns that morning. The muslin day dress made up of gray and lavender had matched her mood — empty, invisible. It ought to have been black, but that would have implied full acquiescence to her new status.

Perhaps that was why she'd acted so out of character.

She'd been a woman between roles.

She hadn't been a wife, in truth. Could she conduct herself as a widow?

Widows were old women with silver hair and sagging skin. Eve nearly groaned.

She'd had intimate relations with her man of business! And this morning, he'd left without a word.

Not that he'd had any choice in the matter. But even so…

Lucy dropped Eve's favorite pelisse onto her shoulders and then handed her a new pair of gloves.

She was a lady. Not a wife. Not a widow,

Not a whore.

She glanced one last time at the bed before closing the door behind her. If she wasn't a whore, what exactly was it that had transpired in that bed last night?

* * *

TWO DAYS LATER, the coach turned up the drive of Pebble's Gate, a home her husband had turned into a place where the devil himself would have felt welcome.

The landscaping had been neglected. This did not surprise her in the least. Jean Luc had spent any funds he controlled on his parties, drink, opium, and whores.

She was saddened to see her own personal garden overrun with weeds. She'd expected no less, but it had been her solace during those last years. Eve blinked away any sentimental memories. She'd begun a new garden behind her London Townhouse. After sorting everything out here, she'd leave once and for all and never return.

But she'd given birth to all three of her daughters here. Some happy memories remained.

The first time she'd entered the house, she'd been filled with innocent dreams.

Dreams.

The word reminded her of what she'd told Niles a few nights ago. That she'd only wanted a kind husband. Had that been a lie? Had she hoped for more than that? Affection? Friendship? Passion?

Had she lowered her expectations of the past in an attempt to squash her disappointment?

She'd not allowed herself much hope for the future. She'd do her best to ensure security. Comfort. She wished to see her daughters thrive. She'd not discouraged her daughters from dreaming.

Her own dreams, however, remained forever in the past. Was passion a dream? Affection?

Eve was a lady of the ton, acquainted with several unmarried older gentlemen, many widowers, who moved within society.

Niles had convinced her she was not without feminine attractions.

Niles.

She'd been unable to dismiss him from her thoughts, despite not having spoken to him since embarking on the remainder of their journey.

He'd made himself scarce since leaving The Goat and Pig, choosing to ride a mount outside instead of inside the carriage with Lucy and herself. Which was to be expected.

Except for his injury. Nobody would have questioned him for riding in the carriage in order to protect his broken ribs.

Perhaps he simply wished to avoid her.

Over the course of the remainder of the trip, he'd ridden ahead of the coach. When they'd catch up, he'd spur his horse and scout the next section of road.

They jolted to a stop, and the vehicle bounced as the outriders hopped off.

The time had come to face Jean Luc's death, in truth.

But when she stepped out and glanced toward the impressive front door, it was her husband's face that peered down at her.

Her knees buckled, and she would have fallen had strong arms not grasped her from behind.

Niles, of course. Had he known? He would have arrived ahead of her.

"Jean Luc?" She forced her gaze to focus on the man of her nightmares.

Only…

The gentleman dashed toward her, arms extended. "Oh, no! I apologize for upsetting you! It's been ages since we last met. I've changed considerably since then, although I cannot say that you have. Aunt Eve, you are as beautiful as ever. In fact, I cannot address you as my aunt. Cousin Eve."

Darius Mossant. Jean Luc's nephew.

Good Lord, but of course he was much younger than Jean Luc. Health and vigor glowed from him. My word, but he looks like Jean Luc did when we married.

Eve shook her head, still relying on Niles' strength. She had not expected the heir to arrive so quickly. Not that it mattered…

"Darius," she finally managed. "You are correct. I believe last I laid eyes on you, you were all of ten years old." A year after her marriage, at his father's funeral. Rhoda had just been born. It was then that Jean Luc had begun his campaign for a son in earnest.

Darius was no longer a boy. Tall, effeminately handsome, and nearly the spitting image of her dead husband.

"Mr. Mossant." Niles reached a hand out in greeting.

Darius did not respond in kind.

"Darius. Please, this is my man of business, indispensable to me for certain, Mr. Niles Waverly. Mr. Waverly, Mr. Darius Mossant. My husband's heir."

Flicking his gaze suspiciously at the other arm with which Niles still grasped her, Darius reluctantly stretched his hand out.

"Mr. Waverly." But then he offered an arm to Eve.

She had no choice but to step away from Niles and take it. Darius was obviously dismissing Niles in doing so. He'd have ignored him but for Eve's introduction. Much as he ignored the driver, the outriders, and Lucy.

A wave of unfamiliar emotions floated through her as Darius escorted her inside.

Disgust. Fear. Repulsion.

Guilt.

She could blame the first three emotions on the similarities between her nephew and Jean Luc's appearance.

The last, she'd rather not dwell upon until she could find time alone.

"Such a tragedy." Darius demanded her attention. "And although there are a few suspects, not a great deal of evidence."

And then a thought struck her.

"When did you arrive?" She'd thought he resided in the north, practically in Scotland. "It's been less than a week." He would have had to have been notified…

"I was visiting Uncle Jean when it happened. He'd asked me to come. Said he had important business to discuss."

But Jean Luc had hated his heir.

"I was under the impression he was hosting a party at the time." Jean Luc had always been hosting some sort of party or another.

Darius opened the door to the front drawing room and escorted her to an unfamiliar loveseat. It ought to be she who invited him inside.

Was she not the mistress still?

But no.

"Has the will been read yet?" Surely Jean Luc's solicitor would have waited until she arrived. She wished Niles had entered with her.

Except he'd not been invited. By Darius, nor by her.

"Not yet." Darius lowered himself to sit beside her. "My uncle's solicitors have yet to arrive from London."

Eve nodded, still trying to understand what was happening. "The roads are not good." Which was an understatement, to say the least. "What did Jean Luc wish to speak with you about?"

Darius's pale eyes shifted toward one of the few paintings that remained. He took a few uneven breaths before answering. "He was concerned about you. It's almost as though he sensed his end was near."

Eve could have laughed if the man wasn't so very serious. What would Jean Luc have wanted to discuss with his heir?

Darius changed the subject, asking after Rhoda and Coleus and Hollyhock. He was aware of Rhoda's marriage. Jean Luc must have told him. Although, he could have read about it. Or heard about it. The marriage and scandal surrounding her oldest daughter's nuptials had created something of a stir. What with the bet and all...

"Miss Coleus will come out this spring then?" The questions sounded innocent enough, but his eyes gleamed with something of a suspicious light.

Eve straightened her spine. "She will not. We'll observe proper morning, of course." She hadn't decided until that very moment. Something protective bringing her maternal instincts to the fore. "If you'll excuse me, I'd like to view the body."

At her request, his gaze settled thoughtfully upon her.

"But of course, Eve."

CHAPTER 12

riends and Relatives

SITTING in the kitchen later that afternoon, Niles wished he'd yanked her away from the pompous ass who'd inherit Jean Luc Mossant's worldly goods.

And the debts, of course. He'd inherit the debts as well. Niles felt not an ounce of sympathy for the bastard.

Instead, he berated himself. At the very least, Niles wished he had insisted upon following them through the damn front door. He didn't like the idea of her being at the mercy of anyone related to her dead husband. He'd wanted to protect her from them.

But Eve had gone willingly inside. It was as though she could not allow herself to acknowledge the time they'd spent together. Of course, she'd been ashamed.

He'd seen the regret in her eyes when she'd ushered her maid into the chamber he'd shared with her for two nights. She'd feared being caught with him — her man of business — an employee. The thought that she was mortified of what they'd done disgusted him.

He'd given her a wide berth ever since. And yes, he himself needed to reestablish his professional position. He'd inspect the estate books for her, sit through the reading of the will, and then depart for London.

She'd mentioned having questions as to the girls' dowries, as well as a trust her father might have insisted be put in place upon her own marriage. In order to discover anything, Niles needed access to those books.

An unwillingness to abandon her now had nothing to do with his decision.

Frustration coursing through him, he pushed back his chair and marched toward the stairs that would lead him to the main part of the house. Niles had tackled situations far stickier than this and knew he'd not find the answer by seeking out the new master.

No, the answers would be found far higher than that. He chuckled to himself.

He needed to locate Jean Luc Mossant's valet.

Two hours and several drinks later, the esteemed gentleman's gentleman sat across from Niles in a nearby pub. Mr. Reginald Forrester, a very ordinary looking gentleman who appeared to be nearing his fifties, hadn't been all that difficult to track down. Niles experienced even less difficulty enticing him to talk about his former master's last dealings.

Jean Luc Mossant hadn't done a great deal to ensure much loyalty, that was for certain. For the price of a few ales, the man would spill the dead man's darkest secrets to a perfect stranger.

"My bet's on Mrs. Donnelly's husband." Mr. Forrester speculated the murder in a conspiratorial tone. "Mossant owed her close to a thousand pounds."

Niles wouldn't ask after the services that might have been rendered. Instead he nodded, keeping a mildly interested expression on his face. "Your master didn't pay his debts?"

The valet threw back his head and laughed heartily. "Not recently. But he had a plan." Without lowering his voice, the valet continued. "Heard that his wife had come into a plump sum of money."

"How'd she manage that? She an heiress?"

"A wager. Bet that her own daughter would sacrifice her virtue." Apparently the valet thought this quite humorous, guffawing and winking. "And she won. The thing is, she and Mossant had been separated so long, a good deal of effort was going to be required to gain access to it."

Efforts which would not have been successful. Those funds were invested under names Mossant never could have uncovered. Niles would know better than anyone. But Mossant would not have known this, and his notions might explain why Mossant had invited his heir. He'd needed someone to assist him in getting to Eve.

Niles scratched his chin. The timeliness of Darius Mossant's visit caused his hair to stand on end.

He recalled the man's smug expression as he'd led Eve into the house. "How did Mossant intend to get it from her?" He remained impassive, as though none of this mattered.

The valet leaned closer. "Was gonna send the heir after it." A snicker. "But he won't have to go after her now. Word is that she's come to pay her respects, showed up at the mansion today. The heir's a handsome devil. I imagine he could win the old girl over. Past her prime for certain."

Niles stifled the impulse to plant a facer on the valet. This was not the time to defend her honor. She'd much prefer he defend her fortune.

In order to do that he needed to get back to Pebble's Gate. It was imperative that she know that her husband's heir was aware of her winnings last year.

"WHAT DO you mean Mrs. Mossant is not available?" Eve wasn't the sort of woman to lie abed throughout the day. "Is she ill?"

The seedy-looking butler shook his head. "She is indisposed at the moment. Would you like to speak with the master?"

Hell yes, he'd speak with the master. "If you would lead me to him." Niles kept calm despite the sick feeling that had settled in the pit of his stomach.

"Of course." The butler would not meet his eyes. For this man to have held onto his employment with someone as disreputable as Jean Luc Mossant for as long as he had, Niles doubted he could be trusted.

What the hell was Darius Mossant up to?

And then a thought struck. What if Eve didn't want to see him? What if she was experiencing so much regret that she could not bring herself to face him?

It was possible Mossant had nothing to do with her inaccessibility after all.

But he'd assume otherwise until she told him herself.

The butler opened the door and gestured for Niles to enter.

"Ah, Mr. Waverly. I've been expecting you." Darius Mossant sat behind a large desk with several papers strewn in front of him. Niles didn't trust the smile, nor the handshake offered. "I imagine you'd like a look at the estate books. You'll discover, unfortunately, that my uncle has burdened me with nothing but a stack of vowels."

"In addition to the estate," Niles added.

At which Mossant chuckled. "Indeed." He lifted a small notebook out of the top drawer and handed it over. "Of course, everything should be settled tomorrow at the reading."

Niles opened the pages and nodded.

"Of course, I'd like to go over these with Eve— with Mrs. Mossant." Dammit! What kind of a fool was he to slip up and say her given name? Amateur move on his part.

Mossant's eyes narrowed at him. Of course, he'd noticed.

"Mrs. Mossant does not wish to be disturbed. As her closest living family member, I'll respect her request. She's had quite a shock and needs her rest. I do believe viewing my uncle's corpse disturbed her more than she expected."

Was the man not aware that she had three daughters? Of course he was. He was simply of a mind to put Niles firmly in his place.

Niles was not family. He was not even a social equal.

He was tempted to argue but was in no position to demand anything. For now, he'd not press the matter. He would find Eve on his own. Regardless of what had gone on between the two of them, he had a duty to perform for her and he'd damn well do it.

"I suppose." Niles slapped the book against his thigh. "You won't mind if I peruse this overnight." Likely, there was nothing to hide. Common knowledge was the estate was buried in debt.

"But of course." The other man rose. Even with Niles' injured ribs, he could take him out, he had no doubt. He stood a good six inches taller and outweighed the heir by at least two stones.

But such action wasn't yet necessary. And of course, Niles did not wish to find himself facing charges, especially away from London, away from the people who would interfere upon his behalf.

"I'll have the butler escort you out."

"Not necessary," Niles rejoined. Of course, the bastard would be aware Niles had spent the previous night in a small chamber above stairs. "If you remember correctly, Mrs. Mossant requested I remain here at Pebble's Gate until matters were settled to her approval."

The smaller, younger man nodded slowly. It seemed that he too, was unwilling to show his hand.

. . .

Eve was staying in the Mistress' chamber. Niles had serendipitously bumped into a maid carrying a dinner tray upstairs and deduced her destination. For now, he stood behind a rather large planter, awaiting the maid to exit.

He'd quickly surmised that most of the servants had been newly hired. The average duration of employment was less than one week. Some had been hired before Jean Luc Mossant's death, and some had been hired after. All had been hired by Darius Mossant.

His instincts screamed that something was off.

Niles ducked down when the made stepped back into the corridor.

And then, without warning, an adjacent door opened and Mossant waved the servant over. "Make certain she eats," he commanded in a cold voice.

The maid nodded, keeping her head down. "I will, sir. She's sleeping now, but I'll check back in soon to see she does as you wish."

"And then report to me," he ordered.

Eve? Sleeping? In the middle of the day? She'd never take anything to calm her nerves. She'd been more than adamant with him regarding her feelings towards such medicines.

As soon as the corridor cleared, Niles stole across the hallway and pushed at the door. At least it wasn't locked.

Careful of being caught, he quickly slipped inside and clicked it shut behind him.

The curtains were drawn closed, leaving a small amount of light for him to see. The high canopied bed was not empty.

"Eve?"

At her lack of response, he cleared his throat and spoke her name again, this time more loudly. "Eve?"

"Jean Luc?" A tiny voice mumbled from beneath the covers. "Please don't. Please don't."

Niles used the conveniently mounted steps to hop up and sit beside her. Upon pulling the covers back, he felt a small sense of relief.

She was sleepy and rumpled, but she seemed unharmed.

"Eve, sweetheart?" He couldn't help himself and reached out to brush away the silky strands covering her face. She wasn't fevered. Perhaps Mossant had simply been stating the truth. She'd undergone a considerable hardship after the accident.

And then been thrown into her past upon arrival at her former home, Pebble's Gate. Where her useless husband's body was laid out.

He himself had viewed the dead husband and it hadn't been pretty.

"Niles?" she mumbled again without opening her eyes. "So tired."

"I know, my dear Mrs. Mossant." He leaned forward and pressed a kiss to her forehead. Likely, she'd thrash him if she were awake. "I needed to check on you. That's part of my job, correct? To make sure you're not in any danger?"

He knew it was not. To be precise, his job was to keep her funds safely tucked away.

"Danger? Jean Luc?" Her eyes fluttered open for only a few seconds. "I don't want to marry him. I donwanna..." Seeing her husband's body would have brought back all manner of recollections.

He needed to tell her about Darius. But would she remember?

If she were anybody else, he'd think she'd taken a dose or two of laudanum.

But she hated it. Said she'd rather die than take any.

"Eve. I need you to listen to me."

"Ummhmm..."

"Your nephew knows about the money from the bet. Jean Luc told him about it."

"Ummhmm…"

"The money is safe, of course. But don't make any decisions or sign anything without me? Can you hear me, Eve? I'm not so certain I trust your nephew."

"Ummhmm…"

Niles sighed. She must be exhausted. Perhaps she hadn't slept the night before. Or the night before that. He certainly hadn't slept a great deal.

"Meet me in the morning after breakfast, yes?" He ran one hand through his hair. The last thing he'd expected was that Mossant had been telling the truth.

Perhaps she had given in and taken a small dose of something but that was difficult for him to believe.

"Niles?"

He'd been about to hop off the bed but turned back to see her sleepy eyes. "Yes, love?"

"Could you? Do you think you might? I never thought it possible…" Her voice sounded weak and thin.

"Could I what?" He leaned forward to hear her better. She sighed softly and closed her eyes again. Niles touched her cheek. "Could I what?"

"Love me?"

Niles swallowed hard before touching his lips to her forehead again.

"I have since I met you." His whispered words were met by silence. Perhaps she hadn't been so ashamed after all. But then, no. He dismissed the thought. She was out of her head with exhaustion. "I'll see you tomorrow love. Rest up."

CHAPTER 13

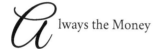lways the Money

"Mrs. Mossant? You must not dally. There's little time to dress."
Eve didn't recognize the nervous voice pulling her from sleep.
"I've hot tea and something for you to eat. Mr. Mossant has
requested you join him in the study in one hour."

The words barely penetrated this fog she couldn't seem to
escape. Mr. Mossant? But Jean Luc was dead.

When had this cloying fog dropped on her? Eve tried to swallow, but her mouth was dry. So dry.

Hands pulled her to sit up and began tugging at her gown. A
woman's hands. A maid. Not Lucy. Where was Lucy? "Come this
way, Missus." The hands assisted her off the bed so that Eve stood
swaying unsteadily.

Her old suite. The one she'd occupied years ago. When she'd
lived with Jean Luc.

Jean Luc. That's when the fog lowered around her. She'd been

ANNABELLE ANDERS

staring at his lifeless corpse contemplating the tragedy of his life. Darius had entered behind her. He'd told her she'd gone pale.

She couldn't remember anything after that. She must have fainted.

And now she could hardly open her eyes. She'd never been one of those squeamish women. Why had she fallen apart then?

And why could she not rouse herself now?

Tea. All she needed was some tea.

Eve fought to open her eyes and took the cup from the unfamiliar maid.

"Where is Lucy?"

"Lucy, ma'am? I wouldn't know who Lucy is. You'll have to ask Mr. Mossant." The maid helped Eve to the bench in front of the vanity and began brushing out her hair. The calming strokes of a brush never failed to soothe her. Eve took another sip and closed her eyes again.

She'd dreamed of Niles. That he'd come to her. Held her and called her his 'love.' Oh, the fog was falling again. Had she fallen asleep sitting here?

"Eve, my love. You look ravishing." A strong arm assisted her to her feet.

Weights seemed to hold her eyelids closed. She wanted to see but hadn't the strength to fight. Where had Jean Luc come from? This man she now leaned upon wasn't Niles.

Niles was taller. Stronger.

Safer.

By her will alone, she barely was able to crack open one eye.

She could make out a few forms, but they were shrouded in the black fog.

"Thank you," she managed, and then gave into the arms holding her up. All she wanted to do was sleep.

* * *

WORRY PLAGUED Niles as he made his way to the study for the reading of the will the next morning. A disquieting thought had struck him in the middle of the night.

Where had Lucy gone? Why hadn't Eve's maid been with her?

Had she taken ill again, herself? She hadn't been well enough to travel initially. Or had she simply been occupied elsewhere?

He'd spent what remained of the night studying the numbers and transactions in the documents provided by Mosssant. Nothing surprising in the accounts. What had interested Niles was the page that had been torn out at the end.

He'd used a piece of charcoal to lift the indentions from the blank page beneath it.

A number had been written boldly and underlined twice. It was the precise amount of Eve's winnings. And Eve's winnings amounted to only three hundred pounds more than the negative number at the end of the ledger.

Regardless of whether the dead Mossant or the live one had written it, one thing was becoming very clear to Niles. The owner of Pebble's Gate believed the answer to all his troubles lay in Eve Mossant.

The door to the study had been propped open, and the room was already mostly occupied. A few servants, including Mr. Forrester, had taken the chairs set back from the desk. Mossant and a woman draped in black, sat behind it.

Eve? Surely it wasn't.

Only it was. He knew that posture. The lovely tilt of her head, but shrouded in black?

"Ah, Mr. Waverly, thank you for coming. We've been waiting for you." The doors closed shut behind him, and Mr. Mercer Priebus, Jean Luc Mossant's personal solicitor, gestured for Niles to take a seat.

Niles glanced at the clock. He'd been told the reading would be at ten in the morning. It was only now nine forty-five.

Mossant sat with a smug look on his face. Of course, he'd told Niles the wrong time.

Eve hadn't so much as angled her head in his direction. Closer now, he could make out her profile, the outline of her lips, and her downcast eyes hidden behind the dark veil.

"Most of this is a mere formality. I'm sorry if any of you have traveled far with hopeful expectations." Mr. Priebus donned a pair of spectacles and continued squashing the few servants' hopes. "Although the deceased made mention of stipends for, ahem, Mr. Reginald Forrester, Mrs. Maude Cooley, Mr. Donald Smith, and a Mr. John Blaycock, the estate's funds have been absorbed by debts incurred by…" And he went on to list a litany of vendors, some reputable and some not so much.

"Mr. Darius Mossant, as the next male in the deceased's line of kin inherits the Pebble's Gate estate and all debt and incomes incurred and generated."

"Mrs. Mossant." The solicitor addressed Eve. "As the deceased's widow, you are welcome to reside at Pebble's Gate at Mr. Darius Mossant's discretion. In the event he decides to evict, a dowager house on the north side of the property shall be opened up and made available."

Niles knew of Eve's plan to reside in London. He looked to her for some response — any response at all. What had happened to the woman he'd known the past year? The woman he'd left here yesterday morning?

"I'd like a word with my client." Niles rose and crossed the room to stand before her. "Mrs. Mossant?" He held out his hand.

"She has no further need of your services, Waverly. Isn't that right, my darling?" Mossant placed one arm around her shoulders. Eve seemed to nod, almost as though moving under water.

Niles dropped to his haunches, taking her hands in his. What in the hell was going on?

"Mrs. Mossant, Eve." He didn't give a God damn at this point what anyone thought. "You haven't any intentions of staying on

94

at Pebble's Gate, do you?" He willed her to raise her chin and tear off the black veil.

"But of course, she's staying on. We're to be married by special license this afternoon."

Oh, hell no.

But why was Eve not making her own denial?

"Is this true?" Niles rubbed her cold hands between his.

"You'll remove your hands from my fiancée."

Again, Eve made no protest.

She might as well have slapped him. Could this be what she wanted?

"What have you done to her?" Niles demanded as burly arms grabbed him from behind. The other servants were already shuffling toward the door, and Mr. Priebus was gathering his papers together.

Darius Mossant clucked his tongue obnoxiously. "Such a shame. She told me everything. How you'd fallen in love with her, taken advantage of her weakened state. I expect all of her personal accounts transferred to me without delay. As her husband, I assure you that Mrs. Mossant shall no longer require your services."

Niles didn't care that the arms clasped around him were crushing his ribs which had not even begun to heal. He threw all his weight forward and managed to make contact with Mossant's chin.

"Get him out of here!" The blighter's hand flew up just in time to catch the tooth that had broken free. The arms around Niles grasped tighter, dragging him out the door.

He was no match for two hefty laborers.

In less than two minutes, they tossed him unceremoniously onto the gravel drive.

Niles stared up at the wispy clouds set against a blindingly blue sky.

He closed his eyes in an attempt to gather his strength. He

was getting too old for this sort of thing.

"Mr. Waverly? What on earth are you doing on the ground?" A familiar voice drew him back to reality.

"Been out drinking, old man?"

Eve's eldest daughter and her husband, the Earl of Carlisle, were both bent over, peering down at him.

Niles had no idea where they'd come from but was happy enough at their timely arrival.

It was all the encouragement he needed to push himself off the ground. And he only groaned a little as he found his feet.

"My Lady." He nodded. "Lord Carlisle. I've reason to believe Mrs. Mossant is in danger." He brushed the gravel from his backside and undertook to explain his suspicions.

"He says mother's agreed to marry him? But that's outrageous!" Lady Carlisle made a move toward the manor, but her husband grasped hold of her arm.

"Rhododendron." The earl halted her charge. "If your mother is in danger, I'll not have you bursting inside. We need the magistrate."

The young woman, who looked so much like her mother, was shaking her head in denial. "But Mama would never agree to marry. Not unless she was in love, and I've met Cousin Darius. Believe me, she is not in love with him. Why on earth is she going along with this?"

"She's been drugged." It was all beginning to make sense to Niles now. "It's the only explanation."

Lady Carlisle wrung her hands together.

"Rhoda." Carlisle turned to his wife. "Fetch Coachman John from the stables and have him take you to find the magistrate."

"Excellent. Meanwhile, Carlisle, you and I can stop the wedding."

Niles had an idea.

The countess nodded. "Be careful, Justin, and you too Mr. Waverly. Don't let her marry him!" She then took off at breakneck speed toward the stables while Niles shared his plan with Lord Carlisle.

"Remember that ship that went down last month? Well…"

CHAPTER 14

If Anyone Has Any Objections…

SHE'D BEEN CAUGHT in a nightmare. Eve wanted to speak up but her thoughts would not connect to her voice. Or her body.

The veil, the darkness. And the fact that two very large brutes had dragged Niles away.

Whose arm was she leaning upon? Niles ought to be beside her. She fought through the heaviness and forced herself to hear the words being read out loud.

The reading of the will?

"…we are gathered together here in the sight of God, and in the face of these witnesses, to join together this man and this woman in holy matrimony; which is an honorable estate, instituted of God in the time of man's innocence…"

A wedding?

Rhoda and Carlisle had married already, hadn't they? Of course, they had. He'd whisked her away… Eve had never been so happy as when Rhoda and Carlisle married.

The man beside her vibrated as he mumbled something...

Eve would be utterly content if Coleus and Holly found themselves husbands with even half as much good character as Lord Carlisle. Even so, if they did not, they'd never worry about security. They could remain with her. Host exhibitions and readings at their home.

She would purchase her home in London now that Jean Luc was gone.

Niles had assured her she'd have no difficulties.

"Marigold Evelyn Mossant." The voice read.

How she hated her given name. Marigold. But then she'd done the same to her own daughters. A hint of a smile touched her lips. She'd protect her daughters with her life. Darius Mossant would never get his hands on Coleus, as he'd hinted. He was too much like his uncle. Too much like Jean Luc. Eve had sensed it after only a few minutes in his presence.

The memory, for some reason, brought her back to the present. She was leaning upon Darius. Not Niles.

And then the words floating around the room began to take shape.

"Wilt thou have this man to thy wedded husband, to live together after God's ordinance in the holy estate of matrimony? Wilt thou obey him, and serve him, love, honor, and keep him in sickness and in health; and, forsaking all other, keep thee only unto him, so long as ye both shall live?"

Silence.

"Eve dear, tell the man yes." That voice, so much like Jean Luc's, sent shivers racing down her spine.

"No." Barely a whisper emerged past her dry lips. She swallowed. Summoning all her strength, she lifted her chin. "No."

"She doesn't mean it." Darius again, trying to silence her now.

"No." She spoke the word again and pushed away from the arm she'd been leaning on.

How had this happened? Hands gripped her elbow so tightly

that it hurt. But she welcomed the pain. Something was very wrong with her.

The tea.

He'd put something in her tea.

Memories of people attending some of Jean Luc's parties, lying about with heavy lids and blanks stares, pressed themselves upon her. The opium.

God help her. She'd been drugged.

"Send for my maid, please." Eve tried to lift the veil away from her face, but her arm was too heavy.

"She's confused."

"I think, perhaps, we ought to wait until Mrs. Mossant is feeling better?" The vicar suggested.

"If you value your position you'll continue with the ceremony."

But the ceremony would, indeed, be delayed.

The heavy door flying open sent Eve jumping. She didn't move far, however, as the hand holding her squeezed even tighter.

It seemed, one of the guests was late to arrive.

Niles.

Even through the veil, she knew it was him in an instant. She'd always recognize his stance, his posture. Like a knight to her rescue, his sturdy frame filled the doorway.

Her man of business, but so much more.

"Pardon my interruption, vicar." Niles sauntered across the room quite unperturbed.

Eve cheered inwardly at the sound of that calm soothing voice she'd come to love.

"The groom has requested some papers from me. I do believe he'll be quite interested to look at them before making any rash decisions."

Eve had no idea what Niles was nattering on about, but it didn't matter.

He was here.

"Explain yourself, Waverly."

Darius loosened her arm to swipe the papers away from Niles, leaving Eve standing on her own. She wavered and then leaned against a chair.

"The investments? Her accounts?"

Niles chuckled softly. Eve felt not one iota of concern that Niles would hand over the information Darius wanted.

"What's left of them."

"What do you mean, what's left of them?" Darius Mossant's voice shook.

And then Eve somehow managed to push the veil over up and over her head. "Yes, what do you mean, what's left of them?" Surely, Niles wouldn't have been careless with her money.

"Sometimes investments pay off." Niles shrugged. "And sometimes, they do not." He didn't look all that worried, or contrite for that matter. He turned to Eve, looking quite adorable despite his alarming announcement. Frustrating man that he was.

"That shipment we discussed, remember? It would have tripled the value of your shares, Mrs. Mossant, and I really hadn't foreseen much risk but..." He shrugged again. "The Estonia went down last month. I'm sure you heard about it. The news has been all over the papers."

But they'd decided not to invest there! Oh!

Oh!

"My money's all gone?" Eve would play along. Her dear, sweet, Mr. Waverly was making all of this up.

"How in the hell am I supposed to afford this damn estate then?" All of the pride and bluster seemed to flee Darius Mossant in that moment as he dropped into a nearby chair.

"You could try learning how to run it properly. A little work never hurt anybody." Lord Carlisle spoke up from the doorway. When had he arrived? If he was here, then surely Rhoda could not be far away.

Niles was by her side now, leading her to the only settee in the room.

"Eve? Look at me sweetheart. Are you all right?" That familiar cultured, yet completely unaffected voice was nearly her undoing. When had her hands begun shaking? Her legs lacked the strength to keep her up even a moment longer, and her stomach had become disturbingly unsettled.

"He gave me opium." She burst into tears. The dawning realization horrified her.

And then she embarrassed herself quite beyond redemption.

Nile's boots would never be the same.

CHAPTER 15

lear Heads Prevail

WITH BOTH EVE and Lucy assisting her up the stairs, Eve wondered that she hadn't realized earlier that she'd been drugged. Even now, she could hardly lift her feet up each step. All that tea she'd drank... Eve shuddered at the thought and turned her mind to eavesdrop on the arguments drifting up from the study. Loud at first, but gradually subsiding as Niles' steady voice took control.

Her mind conjured images of how he'd looked that day in the rain. Catching her from falling, holding her in the shelter of the trees. He'd put her before himself, despite his injury.

The three women shuffled into her chamber and assisted her onto the bed.

Eve didn't want to sleep anymore. She hated this feeling of being trapped within her own body.

"I knew something must be dreadfully wrong, as soon as Mr. Waverly said you intended to marry." Rhoda sat beside the bed and dabbed a cool cloth over Eve's forehead. "Opium! The scoundrel! He had to have known how you opposed the poison!"

"I'll never forgive him for it." Although feeling weak and horribly humiliated, Eve no longer experienced the heavy darkness she'd been subdued by for the past twenty-four hours. Shortly after Eve's...unfortunate bout of sickness, Rhoda had arrived with a magistrate and as luck would have it, Lucy. Apparently, Darius had fired the poor girl. She'd gone into the village and had been looking for Niles.

"Drink this, Mama."

"No tea!" Eve pushed the drink away.

Her daughter's eyes pooled with unshed tears. "It's safe, Mama. I promise. I made it myself." And then Rhoda leaned forward, resting her head on Eve's shoulder.

Rhoda had endured so much already in her young life. Eve hated that she was causing her any duress. Mothers were supposed to comfort their children, not the other way around. "Of course, it is. I'm sorry to worry you."

Eve sipped her tea, relieved at being safe once again. Darius Mossant no longer had any power over her. He never had, in fact. She'd been held captive by the drug.

How had Jean Luc lived his life in such darkness? Had he been imprisoned by the drug all that time?

She'd hated it. It had nearly robbed her of her own free will. And yet... it promised a false comfort.

She now understood its lure. It's power.

Never again. It was horrid and demonic and... terrifying.

Rhoda sat back and wiped an errant tear. "Mr. Waverly certainly is clever," she commented, oh, so casually. Her hands shook a little as she returned the cup of tea to the tray beside the bed.

Eve could only marvel at this brave, beautiful girl. Her daughter!

"Don't you think so?"

Ah, Niles. Clever Niles. "He certainly is."

Eve smiled at the thought that her man of business could so easily command a room full of gentleman whom society would consider his betters.

"You'll have to give him a raise, Mama."

"Give Niles a raise?" Eve nearly laughed. He'd never take it. "He works on commission."

"When we arrived, he was a man possessed. For all of two minutes, he was in quite the panic. I never imagined he could be anything other than utterly calm and composed."

He'd worried for all of two minutes. Again, Eve smiled. She had first-hand knowledge of the hidden passions of Niles Waverly

Eve squirmed and Lucy stepped forward to stuff an extra pillow behind her.

"Thank you, Lucy." Her maid had had a difficult few days as well. "I'm sorry for the trouble you've had. You've been wonderful with the girls since coming on. You certainly didn't deserve such treatment, and I'm sorry I was unable to protect you from it."

THE YOUNG WOMAN was only a few years older than Rhoda.

"I'll be fine. I was just so worried of what they were doing to you. I knew you'd never send me away like that." Lucy twisted her hands together.

"And I never will. You have my word on that." Eve knew that she and her girls were the closest to family Lucy had. Darius Mossant had thought only of himself.

Apparently uncomfortable, Lucy glanced around the room and then asked, "would you care for something to eat, ma'am?"

"Something light, thank you Lucy." Eve wasn't hungry, but the maid seemed to need a moment to herself.

And Eve needed some privacy.

Left alone, Eve could ask her daughter a very personal question. Something she'd been contemplating since the moment she realized she'd nearly married her dead husband's cousin.

"Darling?"

Rhoda's brows rose at her tone and she sat forward attentively. "Yes?"

Eve cleared her throat. "Would you consider me foolish, I mean. Are you happy?" She hedged.

"I am. You know that I am." The somber mood fled her daughter for the moment. Lord Carlisle had been perfect for her. Eve had seen it from the beginning.

"Justin can be at times overly protective, and a bit stuffy." She smiled. "But he's made me happier than I ever might have imagined. Are you happy, Mama?"

How did one discuss something like this with one's daughter? She supposed one discussed it as though she were a friend.

"I think I can be."

"Because father is dead?"

Eve had quite come to terms with her emotions over Jean Luc's death. "Your father's death doesn't make me happy." She explained. "Although, I am relieved. I am also sad. At one time, he was a good man. At one time…"

Rhoda tilted her head. Again, Eve searched for words.

"I'm in love with Niles Waverly." The words rang clear and true. "I didn't think I'd ever feel love again, and I'm uncertain as to whether or not he feels the same…"

A huge grin spread across her daughter's face. "I don't think you need have any fears there."

"You're a Countess now."

At these words, her daughter broke into a peel of laughter. "Oh, Mama. Are you asking for my approval?"

Was that it? "I don't want to make a ninny of myself." This was more embarrassing than she'd imagined. She was past the age of forty!

"Remember what you told me when I didn't know what to do about the bet? Or about Justin?"

Eve remembered. Of course, she remembered. "I do."

"You told me that we Mossant woman oughtn't only to survive, but that we deserved to thrive." Rhoda smiled as she spoke the words.

"I've wanted that for you and for Coleus and Hollyhock more than anything, all along."

"And we want it for you."

Eve simply stared into her daughter's eyes. "I'm so very proud of you."

"Of course, you are," the little imp supplied. "But what of you? Are you going to allow yourself to thrive? Are you going to be able to live your life in faith that good things await you? Or are you going to allow the bad stuff to rule you?"

This daughter of mine. She knows me all too well.

Not waiting for an answer, Rhoda touched the side of her face with one finger as though contemplating something of great import. "Because there is a gentleman downstairs this very minute of whom, I'm certain, would like nothing better than to assure himself of your happiness and well-being."

Eve bit her lower lip.

Rhoda would not relent. "Would you like to see him?"

But she must look a fright! Did it matter? Of course, it mattered!

"After you've done something with my hair." She glanced down at the horrid black gown she'd been dressed in. "And anything but this atrocity. Something bright perhaps? My cerulean?"

Upon which, allowing Eve a glimpse of the tiny little girl she'd once been, her daughter grinned from ear to ear. "I'll have Lucy press it as soon as she returns."

* * *

TWENTY MINUTES LATER, Eve sat in the small sitting area of her suite holding a book. She had no idea what it was about and doubted she ever would.

Rhoda had excused herself to go in search of Niles.

What if he didn't wish to come? What if he was angry with her? From what she'd since learned, Eve had discovered she'd sat mute while Darius Mossant fired him! Her very efficient and most appreciated man of business.

Rhoda had assured her that Mr. Waverly did not hold a grudge.

But what if he did?

And what if he didn't want—

A knock at the door interrupted her misgivings.

"Come in." She set the book aside and smoothed her skirt in her lap. The air seemed to change the second he stepped inside — and the colors in the room — and the weight in her heart.

"I expected you'd remain abed." His voice drew her gaze.

He did not look angry. He simply looked like... Niles. When had he come to mean so much to her? Truth be told, she'd always looked forward to their meetings with considerable anticipation.

"I've spent far too much time abed as of late." At his hesitancy, she gestured beside her. "Won't you sit down?"

Oh, but she felt like a gauche young girl suddenly.

The cushions sank as he lowered himself beside her. And then, instantly alleviating all her concerns, he reached over and covered her hand with one of his.

This wasn't going to be excruciatingly hard, as she'd feared. She drew in a breath. "I—"

"Please, give me a moment first... I need to say something." His voice prevented her from diving headlong into her own practiced speech.

She turned so that she could look him directly in the eye. And as if it was the most natural thing in the world to do, she placed her other hand atop his.

"You will always have my assistance." He cleared his throat. "I'll do anything you need. But I can no longer remain in your employ. I'll protect your assets. I'll protect your daughters. God help me, I'll do better to protect you. But not for payment."

"Surely, you must require some sort of fee?"

His eyes flared at her question.

Oh, but this man. She'd always feel safe beside him. And protected. And desired.

He rubbed his chin. "The only payment I'm willing to accept may be beyond your budget."

Eve could only smile at such foolishness. "I'm a very wealthy woman. That is, of course, unless you did, in fact, send my money to the bottom of the sea," she teased, knowing of course, that he had not.

He waved the concern away. "Never."

But he'd been about to tell her something of import. "Then what is it that I may not be able to afford?" Eve closed her eyes, afraid she'd gotten it all wrong.

"Marriage."

Her eyes flew open at the word. Joy exploded inside her. She had to press her lips together to keep from smiling. "To you?"

"Yes." He nodded in all seriousness. "To me."

"Yes."

"Yes?" He didn't move. "You'll consent to becoming Mrs. Niles Waverly?"

"Aside from my unmarried daughters I've quite used up any goodwill I had for my current name. So, yes. Please." She nodded. "I'd be more than happy to become Mrs. Niles Waverly."

The dear man remained utterly sober. "I'm more than capable of taking care of you. All your funds will remain yours and your daughters'. Always."

He spoke so earnestly. Of course, she knew this about him. "It needn't, you know. I only have one requirement."

"Indeed?" He cocked a rakish eyebrow. Because, yes indeed, her dear Mr. Waverly was quite capable of appearing rakish.

"I expect you to make love to me long and often. And I expect you to allow me to love you."

His throat worked a few times as he swallowed hard. "I never hoped..." Another swallow. "Your love is all I've wanted, Eve. Since I met you. So self-assured you were. So absolutely beautiful. So devoted a mother. I've been in awe of you every day."

"So, I've not been an annoying client?" She could tease him now. He loved her. He had said he loved her, hadn't he?"

"In case you've any doubt, you should know that I retired eight months ago. You're my only client." And then he touched her face, almost in awe. "I love you."

She would not cry. He'd seen her do enough of that for a lifetime. This was a time for laughing and loving and new beginnings.

A second chance for both of them. A second chance at love.

"Aren't you supposed to kiss me now, Mr. Waverly?"

He leaned in and hovered his lips less than an inch from hers. "My dear Mrs. Mossant. I thought you'd never ask.

THE END

FALL IN LOVE with More Sassy Heroines and Dashing Heroes in the Devilish Debutantes Series...

DEVILISH DEBUTANTES SERIES

Hell Hath No Fury

(Devilish Debutante's, Book 1)

Forever a Wallflower... Miss Cecily Findlay practices proper etiquette, dances the waltz flawlessly, wears clothes of the latest fashion, and is a beauty in her own right. Even so, she'd never be received by the ton if not for her enormous dowry...which has attracted Flavion Nottingham, a spoiled and entitled earl. This so called gentleman has beggared his estate and sees Cecily as the answer to all his problems. Most dastardly of all, he doesn't care if he shatters her dreams while executing his devious scheme.

Forever the Spare... Mr. Stephen Nottingham, successful industrialist, is back in England to save his cousin's (ahem) assets, but may have arrived too late. The clean-up involves settling massive debts, dismissing a clinging mistress, and dealing with more than one irate papa. None of that matters, however, as much as saving the beautiful Cecily.

A Forever kind of Love... Cecily is trapped by Lord Kensington and Stephen is trapped by his honor. Happily ever after hangs in the balance. Will fate open the doors for their enduring love?

HELL IN A HAND Basket

(Devilish Debutante's, Book 2)

Sophia Babineaux has landed a husband! And a good one at that!

Lord Harold, the second son of a duke, is kind, gentle, undemanding.

Perhaps a little too undemanding?

Because after one chance encounter with skilled rake, Captain Devlin Brooks, it is glaringly obvious that something is missing between Lord Harold and herself... pas-sion... sizzle... well... everything. And marriage is forever!

Will her parents allow her to reconsider? Absolutely not.

War hero, Devlin Brookes, is ready to marry and thinks Sophia Babineaux might be the one. One itsy bitsy problem: she's engaged to his cousin, Harold.

But Devlin knows his cousin! and damned if Harold hasn't

been coerced into this betrothal by the Duke of Prescott, his father.

Prescott usually gets what he wants.

Devlin, Sophia and Harold conspire to thwart the duke's wishes but fail to consider a few vital, unintended consequences.

Once set in motion, matters quickly spiral out of control!

Caught up in tragedy, regret, and deceit Sophia and Devlin's love be-comes tainted. If they cannot cope with their choices they may never find their way back once embarking on their journey... To Hell in a Hand Basket...

Hell's Belle

(Devilish Debutante's, Book 3)

There comes a time in a lady's life when she needs to take matters into her own hands...

A Scheming Minx

Emily Goodnight, a curiously smart bluestocking – who cannot see a thing without her blasted spectacles – is raising the art of meddling to new heights. Why leave her future in the hands of fate when she's perfectly capable of managing it herself?

An Apathetic Rake

The Earl of Blakely, London's most unattainable bachelor, finds Miss Goodnight's schemes nearly as intriguing as the curves hidden beneath her frumpy gowns. Secure in his independence, he's focussed on one thing only: evading this father's manipulating ways. In doing so, ironically, he fails to evade the mischief of Emily's managing ploys.

Hell's Bell Indeed

What with all the cheating at parlor games, trysts in dark closets, and nighttime flights to Gretna Green, complications arise. Because fate has limits. And when it comes to love and the secrets of the past, there's only so much twisting one English Miss can get away with...

. . .

Hell of a Lady

(Devilish Debutante's, Book 4)

Regency Romance between an angelic vicar and a devilish debutante: A must read if you love sweet and sizzle with an abundance of heart.

The Last Devilish Debutante

Miss Rhododendron Mossant has given up on men, love, and worst of all, herself. Once a flirtatious beauty, the nightmares of her past have frozen her in fear. Ruined and ready to call it quits, all she can hope for is divine intervention.

The Angelic Vicar

Justin White, Vicar turned Earl, has the looks of an angel but the heart of a rake. He isn't prepared to marry and yet honor won't allow anything less. Which poses something of a problem... because, by God, when it comes to this vixen, a war is is waging between his body and his soul.

Scandal's Sweet Sizzle

She's hopeless and he's hopelessly devoted. Together they must conquer the ton, her disgrace, and his empty pockets. With a little deviousness, and a miracle or two, is it possible this devilish match was really made in heaven?

Hell Hath Frozen Over

(Devilish Debutantes, Novella)

The Duchess of Prescott, now a widow, fears she's experienced all life has to offer. Thomas Findlay, a wealthy industrialist, knows she has not. Can he convince her she has love and passion in her future? And if he does, cans she convince herself to embrace it?

CHAPTER 16

A SAMPLE FROM

HELL OF A LADY

A Most Outrageous Wager

White's Betting Book: 1824, April 7th

- Betts placed below naming whom Miss R.M. will next bestow S. favors upon.
- Minimum. Bett L 1000
- Proof must be provided. Wager open until confirmed.

- April 7th Ld. Mimms, L 1000 on FN (Ld. K)
-April 8th L 2000 Ld. FN (Ld. K)
-April 8th RS (Ld. Q) L 1000 on DB (Ld. W)
-April 8th Ld. Bn.L 1000 on … RY Ld T,
And so forth… And so on…

CHAPTER ONE

 *rabtree Ball*

"I don't understand it, Emily! It's not as though I'm any different this year. I'm the same person I've always been. Heaven knows my dowry's as small as it ever was." Normally, Rhoda wasn't one to question good fortune, but the past year had turned her into something of a skeptic.

For upon her wrist, attached to the string her mother had tied earlier, Miss Rhododendron Mossant possessed a full dance card for the first time in all of her ten and nine years. Not once since coming out two years ago had she ever had more than a third accounted for.

Tonight, a masculine name was scribbled onto every single line.

"Likely something to do with you garnering Lord St. John's notice last year. If a marquess finds you interesting..." Her friend and fellow wallflower, Emily, scrunched her nose and twisted her lips into a wry grimace.

The gentlemen of the *ton*, usually oblivious to her presence, had pounced upon Rhoda the moment she set foot in the ballroom, vying to place their names upon her card. Once they'd procured a set, a few even requested sets with Emily, although with less enthusiasm.

Rhoda had not gone out of her way to flirt or fawn. She hadn't been nearly as friendly as she'd been in the past. So, why now? The question niggled at her as she bent down to adjust her slipper.

The supper dance was next to commence, and her feet already ached. She hadn't prepared to partake in such vigorous exercise this evening. Nor had her life prepared her to be the belle of the ball.

"Miss Mossant."

Rhoda peeked up to identify the owner of the polished boots

that appeared before her. The voice sounded familiar, but she didn't immediately recognize the rather fine-looking gentleman executing a stiff and formal bow.

As she sat upright again, a flush crept up her neck and into her cheeks. Rhoda usually didn't forget a handsome face. Blond hair, blue eyes, perhaps nearing the age of thirty. Ah, yes!

"Mr. White." Mr. Justin White, *the vicar*. She stopped herself from gasping. She'd not met with him since the day Lord Harold died last summer at Priory Point, easily one of the worst days of her life.

Second only to the day she'd been informed of St. John's tragic demise. She shivered as she pushed the thought aside.

"Please, sit down." She indicated the chair Emily had vacated. Rhoda glanced around the room. Where had she gone?

Not much time presented itself for conversation as the next set was soon to begin. She'd promised this one to Flavion Nottingham, the Earl of Kensington, of all people. She could endure the vicar's company until Kensington came to claim her. Mr. White was a *vicar*, after all. One could not simply *ignore* a vicar.

He smiled grimly and lowered himself to the seat. "I trust you are doing well." He cleared his throat. If he felt as uncomfortable as she, then why had he approached her?

Likely, he felt the need to inquire as to her spiritual health. The collar he wore set him quite apart from the other more ornately dressed gentlemen.

And as for the condition of her spiritual health?

She would have laughed, but if she were to begin laughing, it might turn to hysteria. And quite possibly, she'd be unable to stop.

She wasn't sure her soul would ever be *well* again. Not since that weekend Harold had fallen off the cliff. And less than a fortnight later, when a river of mud and rain had swept the steep narrow road near Priory Point into the sea, along with the

Prescotts' ducal carriage. St. John, his father, and uncle had all been riding inside.

"I am well. And you, Mr. White?" She studied him from beneath her lashes. He'd been witness to Harold's death that day, too. The men were all cousins, from what she remembered. Mr. White had nearly jumped into the sea to rescue poor Harold. He'd remained hopeful longer than anyone else. Even longer than Harold's own brother.

Mr. White's persistence might have had something to do with his faith.

"It has been a trying winter," the vicar answered. "But with springtime always comes hope." He spoke sincerely. No mockery in his words whatsoever.

Hope was something she'd given up on. The greater a person's hope, the more pain one experienced when disappointment set in. No springtime for her, just one long, endless winter.

"Is it presumptuous of me to hope I might claim a set with you?"

Her heart fluttered ever so weakly. This handsome, kind, wholesome man showing interest in her... Laughable, really. She smothered any pleasure she'd normally have enjoyed upon his request.

Likely whatever had come over the rest of them affected him as well.

"I'm afraid, sir, they have all been spoken for." When his eyebrows rose in surprise, she held out her wrist. She could hardly believe it herself. "I'm not fibbing, Mr. White! I wouldn't lie to a vicar!"

He shook his head, not bothering to examine the card. Instead, he stared down at his hands, clasped together at the space between his knees. His blond hair, longer than was fashionable, fell forward, hiding his profile from her gaze.

"I am to be disappointed, then." He spoke as though mocking himself but then sent her a sideways glance.

"Hope does that." She couldn't hold back her opinion. "Eventually."

He held her stare solemnly. "I would not have taken you for such a cynic, Miss Mossant."

She turned to watch a few ladies promenading around the room. "Disappointment does that, you know. Too many letdowns tend to stifle one's optimism."

He scratched his chin. Perhaps she confounded him. She certainly wasn't engaging in typical ballroom conversation. She ought to be flirting. Complimenting him, widening her eyes, and feigning enthusiastic agreement with all his opinions.

"I'll wager you're an optimist." She'd redirect the conversation back to him. "A man of God. Your prayers are likely given top priority." She stretched her lips into a smile.

He did not smile back. Again, that sideways glance. Her heart jumped at the startling blue of his eyes.

"I seriously doubt it works that way, Miss Mossant."

"It's not an insult." She'd be certain he hadn't taken her comment that way. "Rather the opposite, really." Those who were good deserved to have their prayers answered. He was obviously one of the good ones. At this thought, she remembered the desperation with which he'd climbed down the side of the cliff, hoping to save Harold.

Hope had driven him. Even then.

And he'd been disappointed. As they all had been.

He cleared his throat. "I'd like to think God does not favor any one of us over others. Are we not all undeserving? Are we not all sinners?"

"Some more than others." She could not be in complete agreement with him. People discriminated. They passed judgment upon one another, upon themselves. And they were made in God's image, were they not?

She met his gaze steadily and shook her head.

"You believe me naïve?" He raised his brows.

"I believe your faith gives you confidence. And your good-ness." Neither of which she could lay claim to. "But I suppose that is why you wear the collar. A true calling."

Those blue eyes of his narrowed. "I hope someday you allow yourself to hope again. You are far too young to be so cynical." His gaze, after searching her face, dropped to her bodice. "And too beautiful."

She shivered. Her lack of hope had nothing to do with her age or her looks. Rather to the circumstances life had handed her. She would not thank him for the compliment. "And you a vicar," she scoffed, feeling defensive at his comment. She didn't like feeling vulnerable, and he'd somehow caused her to feel just that. Why had he chosen to sit *here*? What did he want?

He turned his gaze downward again, and, as though she'd voiced her thoughts, seemed to decide it was time he stated his purpose.

"I do not wish to bring to mind unhappy memories, Miss Mossant." He remained focused on the floor. "But I never had the chance to tell you how much I admired your composure and compassion on that dreadful day. I do not know that your friend could have endured it without your strength and comfort. I've often wanted to tell you this, and when I realized you were here tonight..." His throat worked as he swallowed what else he might say.

His words surprised her.

Again.

She barely remembered the accident itself, often dwelling instead upon everything that happened afterward.

Their assembled group had been sitting atop the cliff, drinking wine and sharing a lovely picnic. Rhoda had been upset with St. John's attention to another lady. Today, she could not even recall the woman's name. Her presence, however, had mattered greatly at the time.

Lord Harold had been in a good-humored mood as he joked about falling into the sea, and St. John had goaded him, it seemed.

And then it was not a joke anymore. "It was all so senseless," she said through lips that felt frozen.

Lord Harold had lost his balance and tumbled over the edge of the cliff. He'd been standing there, laughing one moment, and the next, he'd simply disappeared. He'd ceased to exist.

His wife of less than a fortnight, Sophia, had lurched forward, as though she would jump into the crashing waves below to save him.

Yes, Rhoda had caught her friend, held her back as Sophia sobbed and cried out her husband's name.

"She is my friend," Rhoda added into his silence. "I would do anything for her." And she had. *God save my soul.*

What else was there to say?

"Miss Mossant, my set, I believe." The words crashed into her thoughts almost violently.

Dressed in a cream-colored jacket and an embroidered turquoise waistcoat, the Earl of Kensington could not be more dissimilar to the vicar. His breeches were practically molded to his thighs, and she thought that perhaps he wore padding beneath his stockings. The heels on his buckled shoes would ensure that he stood taller than her, despite her own above-average height.

Rhoda had wanted to refuse him, but in doing so would have had to decline other offers as well. A lady could not deny such a request. Not if she wished to dance with any others that night.

Rhoda twisted her mouth into a welcoming smile.

Her friend Cecily wasn't here. Regardless, she'd understand.

The despicable earl had lied and tricked Cecily into marrying him, and then betrayed her in the worst possible manner. Rhoda knew he was not to be trusted. And yet, here he stood, all affability, affluence, and charm.

Although Kensington had paid for his misdeeds, Rhoda could

never forgive what he'd done to one of her best friends. Even tonight, he'd put Rhoda in an uncomfortable position. He should not have claimed a dance with her. He ought to have remained in the country with his new wife and baby.

If she refused him, she'd be forced to sit all other dances out.

Might as well get this over with.

She turned to Mr. White and nodded. "If you'll excuse me, sir."

She rose hastily, uneasy with the emotions the vicar evoked.

He remained sitting, unwilling, it seemed, to remove himself from the memory they had been reliving together. Scrutinizing her, he nodded, almost imperceptibly.

Regret caught at her to leave their conversation unfinished. She brushed it away. The past must remain in the past. For all of their sakes.

She dipped her chin, signaling the end of their conversation.

Placing one hand on Lord Kensington's arm, she allowed herself to be whisked onto the dance floor for the lively set. Taking her position, she determined to forget the unnerving encounter with Mr. White. She ought to be having the time of her life!

"Your looks are even more dazzling tonight than ever." Lord Kensington stood across from her. His compliment only reminded her of what he'd done to Cecily.

"Thank you." She'd appear sullen and prideful if she failed to respond. And others were watching them. Both the ladies and the gentlemen.

The music commenced, and he reached across the gap to take her hand. Thank heavens they wore gloves. Her skin might have crawled if she'd had to endure the touch of his flesh.

She wished he'd not singled her out this evening.

Dancers all around her smiled and laughed as they executed the well-known steps. Several ladies' gazes followed her partner covetously. Despite his despicable past, no one could deny Lord Kensington was a most handsome and charismatic gentleman.

Initially, as they executed the steps of the dance, he kept his distance and did not attempt to hold her gaze for longer than was considered appropriate. The second time they came together, however, his hand lingered at her waist, and he brushed too close to her body for comfort.

"I cannot identify your scent, Miss Mossant." He leaned his face into her neck. "Roses? But there is a hint of something else? Your own particular magic? Are you casting spells?"

The words struck her as more of an accusation than anything else. She did her best to widen the gap between them. His flirtatiousness set her skin crawling. He persisted in closing the distance between them and leaving his hand on her longer than necessary.

She hoped no one else noticed.

A lady's reputation was all she had.

Except, he was an earl. Surely, he wouldn't do anything to dishonor her in public. He'd mended his ways. Or so everyone said—and by everyone she meant the *ton*.

A time or two, she spotted Mr. White watching them with a scowl. Obviously, he disapproved. Of her? Or of her dance partner?

The question needled.

She barely knew Mr. White. She hoped to never speak with him again, as a matter of fact. They had shared one afternoon, one tragic afternoon together, and each time she saw him, the terrible emotions of that day would resurface. Such a phenomenon did not lend itself to friendship.

Lord Kensington caught her gaze, and she stretched her lips into a smile. She'd always loved dancing, moving to the music, talking and flirting with those around her.

Tonight, she merely endured it. She wished for nothing more

than to return home, change into her night rail, and climb under her counterpane.

The music slowed to a halt. One dance over, two left in the set.

Lord Kensington tucked her arm into his, his face flushed and eyes bright. "My dear Miss Mossant, it's ever so hot in here. Shall we forgo the remainder of the set and take some air?" Without allowing her to answer, his hold upon her elbow tightened, and he led her toward the terrace.

When he went to set his hand at her back, she arched forward. She did not welcome his overly familiar touch.

Lord Kensington's scent clawed at her. At one point, a lifetime ago, she'd considered him desirable, indeed. Now he stirred only disgust in her. She knew him for who he was.

But he was an earl, an influential one, and for that reason, he would never be turned away by society.

Despite the scandalous duel that had grievously injured his... male parts.

"How is Daphne, er, Lady Kensington?" She'd remind him of the lady he'd ended up married to.

No need to flutter her eyelashes at him or encourage his preening boastfulness. Even though that was what gentlemen wanted. They wanted to feel their superiority. It was at least half of what made a man feel worthy.

"My countess is well," he answered tersely.

"And your baby daughter?"

He grimaced but did not answer, unusually intent, it seemed, on steering her away from the ballroom guests.

She had no need to be wary of the earl. She reminded herself that she had nothing to fear. Flavion Nottingham was no longer, in truth, a man. So, why was she suddenly feeling so uncomfortable?

Her mother had attended the ball and would be seated with

the other matrons. Would Rhoda be overreacting if she demanded that he take her back inside?

But, no, Kensington was harmless.

He guided them away from the terrace and down a dark path. In the distance, she caught sight of a tall fountain surrounded by lanterns. Was it an angel or a devil? An odd work of art for such a pretty setting. Water shot up from the wings, and mist hovered around the stone creature.

She shivered to think an angel could appear satanic, as well as the opposite.

People were like that, too.

With an invisible moon, stars twinkled dimly in a mostly black sky, making for a very dark night. Furthermore, the glow of the candles inside the ballroom failed to illuminate much through the windows. Rhoda shivered as the earl's arm slid around her waist.

His breath blew hot behind her ear. "Much better, don't you think?"

Much better for what? The air? Was that what he referred to, the fresh air?

She doubted it. His too-familiar touch sent a shiver of fear creeping along her spine. "I'm fine. Nonetheless, my lord, I wish to return inside now." She must return to her mother. She slowed her pace and resisted him at last. She ought not to have come outside alone like this.

He chuckled but held fast to her, his grip becoming almost painful. "Ah, so, you wish to pretend reluctance, Miss Mossant? Does that make you feel more like a lady?" His words confused her, but his tone set her heart racing in fear.

Without warning, he spun her in his arms and dragged them both off the path, behind one of the tall hedges.

And then hard, cold lips landed on hers.

Stunned, Rhoda pushed against his chest and twisted her head. The taste of whiskey and cigars evoked a wave of nausea.

"Don't play games with me." He was stronger than he looked. One arm held her in place, and the other hitched her skirt higher. "I have too much to gain."

How had this happened? In the matter of a few seconds, she'd gone from casually strolling through the Countess of Crabtree's garden to fighting off a vicious attack! She kicked out at him, but as her slippers encountered his boots, realized the futility of such a strategy.

"Stop it, my lord!" she tried imploring him. Perhaps she had been too passive, allowing him to touch her as he had throughout the dance. Had he thought she *wanted* him to do this? "My lord, stop! Please! I don't want—" His mouth smothered her pleas.

Real panic set in. The earl's hand was now clutching at her bare leg. "Ah, yes, you like a little fight, eh?" He ground their teeth together. Rhoda didn't know if the blood she tasted was his or her own.

Why would he do this? Surely, he couldn't expect any gratification? At that moment, it didn't matter that he lacked the necessary equipment. His hands roved over her arms, and he sought to touch her intimately. Rhoda squirmed and pushed at him, crying, angry and terrified at the same time.

***

Justin had resented Kensington for the set he'd reserved with Miss Mossant. He'd seen the look in Kensington's eyes even before the dance began—a lasciviousness that belied any good intentions.

Perhaps Justin identified it so easily because of his own improper inclinations toward her.

Watching the dancers turn and step to the cheerfully paced music, Justin admitted that he'd been attracted to her the first time they'd met but then been disappointed upon hearing St.

John's boasts. He hadn't wanted to allow his cousin's words to dictate his opinion, but was human, after all.

His gaze searched the dancers making turns about the parquet floor and inexorably settled on the chestnut-haired beauty again. Miss Mossant did not appear excessively flirtatious, but she didn't shun Kensington's advances either. After the first dance of the set ended, the bounder led her off the floor and toward the doors that opened to the terrace. As they disappeared, she put up no argument.

Justin gazed into his glass. He was not mistaken, she considered him naïve. He'd heard it in her voice.

But if she knew his thoughts, she would not think him so benevolent. Even now, his imagination ignored his conscience.

If she'd go walking alone in the dark with *him*... He shook his head, dismissing his untoward thoughts.

When the second dance of the set commenced, a few matrons were tittering and pointing at him with interest. God, he hoped news of his recent inheritance hadn't been made public yet. He'd prefer to bide a few more days in anonymity.

Damn. They looked to be heading his way... with purposeful intent.

Before he could be cornered, he placed his wine on a sideboard and then slipped through the French doors. The air outside the ballroom met him in a refreshing gust. Perhaps he could make his departure with the hostess being none the wiser.

The door closed behind him and he didn't look back to see if the matrons would be so bold as to follow.

His collar scratched uncomfortably. It hadn't done that before. He'd always felt more than comfortable wearing it. Guilt, likely.

Jamming his hands into his pockets, he turned onto a poorly lit pathway. What the devil? Rustling sounds stirred from behind a barrier of foliage. Likely, he had nearly stumbled upon a tryst.

"Does that make you feel more like a lady?" snarled a gruff-sounding voice from the dark area off the path.

Justin crept closer. If this wasn't a consensual encounter, he'd feel compelled to intervene. Not that he was a confrontational man. As a vicar, he'd learned to stifle violent impulses that came over him. He preferred using words to settle most disputes.

He'd also learned, however, that without a willingness to use his fists, talking could be futile.

In an ideal world, neither would be necessary. Hopefully, his suspicions would be proven wrong and he could return inside to finish his wine.

More rustling, and then all of his senses came alert. "Stop it, my lord! My lord, stop! Please! I don't want—"

Miss Mossant's voice. Apparently, she'd issued an invitation she wasn't willing to entertain in full. But she sounded distraught, frantic. Justin lengthened his stride until he came even with the couple. He could barely make out two shadowy figures.

Dash it all, she appeared to be resisting the earl. Yes, the situation had turned ugly indeed.

Although he'd heard rumors of the earl's infamous history, he'd never been introduced. According to most of the *ton*, Kensington had been something of a rake before his emasculating injury. Obviously, the extent of it had been exaggerated. Otherwise, the man would lack the motivation that seemed to have overcome him with Miss Mossant.

What would members of the *ton* think if they knew the extent of debauchery practiced by some of their beloved so-called gentlemen?

The scene before him did not appear consensual.

Justin tensed. "The lady has asked you to stop, Kensington. I suggest you honor her request."

Kensington stilled for a moment upon hearing Justin's words. "Walk away, Vicar. You know nothing of these matters."

Hell and damnation. Justin took one step forward, but before he could grab hold of the bounder's collar, Miss Mossant lifted her knee and landed it with surprising accuracy. The earl stumbled back and then bent over forward, gasping.

Although Kensington deserved it and would receive no pity nor assistance from Justin, his own dangling parts retreated considerably at the thought of experiencing a similar blow.

It seemed he'd not have to bruise his knuckles after all.

Miss Mossant met his gaze, a combination of fear and anger burning in eyes that looked almost black. Her lower lip trembled, and she hugged her arms in front of herself protectively.

With a moan, Kensington dropped to the ground and curled himself into a ball.

What this situation required, Justin assessed, was finesse.

To prevent Miss Mossant from becoming the subject of yet more gossip, he needed to lead her away from watchful eyes, to someplace where she might repair herself. An alluring array of chestnut curls had escaped her coiffure, tumbling down her back. More troublesome, her dress appeared disheveled and had torn in one place. A trickle of blood dripped from her swollen lips.

His gut clenched at the sight.

Justin stepped around Kensington to where Miss Mossant stood frozen. She nearly collapsed before he took hold of her arm. As unobtrusively as possible, he tugged her bodice back into place and then dabbed his handkerchief at her lips. Although his hands were steady, his heart raced.

"Remind me never to anger you, Miss Mossant."

She didn't laugh, blink, or respond in any way to his attempt to break through her lifeless trance.

Others strolled nearby, at a distance of fewer than twenty yards.

Maneuvering her so that she would be indistinguishable in his shadow, he tucked her hand through his arm and led them along the veranda away from the ballroom entrance. They had no choice but to pass a few other guests.

"Is everything all right there?" a tall, elderly gentleman turned away from his companion to inquire.

"Positively delightful evening for a stroll." Justin nodded toward the couple standing near one of the large potted plants. He blocked them from getting a good look at Miss Mossant. "My Lady, My Lord,"

Tall glass-paned doors beckoned at the far end of the terrace, and from what Justin could remember, they led into one of the Crabtrees' drawing rooms. With any luck, the doors would be unlocked and the room empty.

He steered the passive young lady in that direction and released the breath he was holding when the door swung open. Miss Mossant stepped inside but then stood unmoving while Justin lit a few of the candles.

"An unusually dark night." Best to burn only a few. He didn't plan on remaining here long. Just enough time for Miss Mossant to gather her calm so that he could escort her to a ladies' retiring room.

Her stillness gave him pause. Caramel eyes stared straight ahead, unblinking. She wasn't trembling or shaking, but she seemed frozen from the inside.

Justin could have gazed upon her silhouette all night long. If he were that sort of fellow, that was. He turned away from her and examined a painting placed at eye level. She needed a moment. He'd give her a level of privacy to compose herself.

The urge to comfort her, to hold her tightly against him, was strong. But with a woman such as she, his initial desire would hastily be replaced by another, less platonic one.

He was a man of the church, but a man, nonetheless.

But that would make him no better than Kensington.

Finally, the rustling of her skirts signaled that she'd cast off whatever spell she'd been under and had crossed farther into the room. Perhaps she was ready to face him now.

When he turned and caught sight of her expression, he tried to interpret her thoughts. Finely arched brows lowered in concentration, and she seemed baffled. Confused. "I–I thank you for your most timely arrival, Mr. White. I cannot imagine... If you hadn't come along..." Her hands fluttered.

A shiver ran through her, and he glanced around for a quilt. "Are you cold?"

She shook her head.

And then her soulful eyes widened to stare at him. "I must find my mother! She'll be worried if she doesn't see me at supper." The mysterious beauty went to take a step but caught herself on the back of a chair when her knees nearly buckled. "I..."

When he moved to assist her again, she stayed him with one hand, grimaced, and then seemed to shake off her confusion. Moving slower this time, she lifted her skirt as though she'd carefully pick her way to the exit.

Justin seized her by the arm. "First, the retiring room, I think." If she were to reenter the ballroom in her present condition, her ruination would be complete. He held her gaze steadily, making certain she understood his meaning.

Comprehension dawned, and she nodded slowly. "Yes. Yes, of course." At least the corridor wasn't well lit. "Thank you, Mr. White." Shaking him off, she turned again to leave.

"Miss Mossant?" He stopped her with his voice this time. "You would do well to avoid such circumstances in the future. Not all men are so easily thwarted." She really was too beautiful, too *sensual,* for her own good.

Her jaw tightened but she did not meet his gaze again. She nodded. "I am ever so grateful for your kind advice."

And then she was gone.

ABOUT THE AUTHOR

Married to the same man for over 25 years, I am a mother to three children and two Miniature Wiener dogs After owning a business and experiencing considerable success, my husband and I got caught in the financial crisis and lost everything; our business, our home, even our car.

At this point, I put my B.A. in Poly Sci to use and took work as a waitress and bartender. Unwilling to give up on a professional life, I simultaneously went back to college and obtained a degree in Energy Management. And then the energy market dropped off.

And then my dog died. I can only be grateful for this series of unfortunate events, for, with nothing to lose and completely demoralized, I sat down and began to write the romance novels which had until then, existed only my imagination. I am happy to have found my place in life. Finally.

Ms. Anders loves to hear from readers! Please contact her at: www.annabelleanders.com or any of the social media links below!

Twitter

www.annabelleanders.com

Devilish Debutantes Series

Hell Hath No Fury

(Devilish Debutante's, Book 1)

To keep the money, he has to keep her as well…

Cecily Nottingham has made a huge mistake.

The marriage bed was still warm when the earl she thought she loved crawled out of it and announced that he loved someone else.

Loves. Someone else.

All he saw in Cecily was her dowry.

But he's in for the shock of his life, because in order to keep the money, he has to keep her.

With nothing to lose, Cecily sets out to seduce her husband's cousin, Stephen Nottingham, in an attempt to goad the earl into divorcing her. Little does she realize that Stephen would turn out to be everything her husband was not: Honorable, loyal, trustworthy…Handsome as sin.

Stephen only returned to England for one reason. Save his cousin's estate from financial ruin. Instead, he finds himself face to face with his cousins beautiful and scorned wife, he isn't sure what to do first, strangle his cousin, or kiss his wife. His honor is about to be questioned, right along with his self-control.

Amid snakes, duels and a good catfight, Cecily realizes the game she's playing has high stakes indeed. There are only a few ways for a marriage to end in Regency England and none of them come without a high price. Is she willing to pay it? Is Stephen? A 'Happily Ever After' hangs in the balance, because, yes, love can conquer all, but sometimes it needs a little bit of help.

Hell in a Hand Basket

(Devilish Debutante's, Book 2)

Sophia Babineaux has landed a husband! And a good one at that!

Lord Harold, the second son of a duke, is kind, gentle, undemanding.

Perhaps a little too undemanding?

Because after one chance encounter with skilled rake, Captain Devlin Brooks, it is glaringly obvious that something is missing between Lord Harold and herself… pas-sion… sizzle… well… everything. And marriage is forever!

Will her parents allow her to reconsider? Absolutely not.

War hero, Devlin Brookes, is ready to marry and thinks Sophia Babineaux might be the one. One itsy bitsy problem: she's engaged to his cousin, Harold.

But Devlin knows his cousin! and damned if Harold hasn't been coerced into this betrothal by the Duke of Prescott, his father.

Prescott usually gets what he wants.

Devlin, Sophia and Harold conspire to thwart the duke's wishes but fail to consider a few vital, unintended consequences.

Once set in motion, matters quickly spiral out of control!

Caught up in tragedy, regret, and deceit Sophia and Devlin's love becomes tainted. If they cannot cope with their choices they may never find their way back once embarking on their journey… To Hell in a Hand Basket…

Hell's Belle

(Devilish Debutante's, Book 3)

There comes a time in a lady's life when she needs to take matters into her own hands…

A Scheming Minx

Emily Goodnight, a curiously smart bluestocking – who cannot see a thing without her blasted spectacles – is raising the art of meddling to new heights. Why leave her future in the hands of fate when she's perfectly capable of managing it herself?

An Apathetic Rake

The Earl of Blakely, London's most unattainable bachelor, finds Miss Goodnight's schemes nearly as intriguing as the curves hidden beneath her frumpy gowns. Secure in his independence, he's focussed on one thing only: evading this father's manipulating ways. In doing so, ironically, he fails to evade the mischief of Emily's managing ploys.

Hell's Bell Indeed

What with all the cheating at parlor games, trysts in dark closets, and nighttime flights to Gretna Green, complications arise. Because fate has limits. And when it comes to love and the secrets of the past, there's only so much twisting one English Miss can get away with...

Hell of a Lady

(Devilish Debutante's, Book 4)

Regency Romance between an angelic vicar and a devilish debutante: A must read if you love sweet and sizzle with an abundance of heart.

The Last Devilish Debutante

Miss Rhododendron Mossant has given up on men, love, and worst of all, herself. Once a flirtatious beauty, the nightmares of her past have frozen her in fear. Ruined and ready to call it quits, all she can hope for is divine intervention.

The Angelic Vicar

Justin White, Vicar turned Earl, has the looks of an angel but the heart of a rake. He isn't prepared to marry and yet honor won't allow anything less. Which poses something of a problem... because, by God, when it comes to this vixen, a war is is waging between his body and his soul.

Scandal's Sweet Sizzle

She's hopeless and he's hopelessly devoted. Together they must conquer the ton, her disgrace, and his empty pockets. With a little deviousness, and a miracle or two, is it possible this devilish match was really made in heaven?

Hell Hath Frozen Over

(Devilish Debutantes, Novella)

The Duchess of Prescott, now a widow, fears she's experienced all life has to offer. Thomas Findlay, a wealthy industrialist, knows she has not.

Can he convince her she has love and passion in her future? And if he does, cans she convince herself to embrace it?

To Hell And Back

(Devilish Debutantes, Novella)

Eve Mossant's life has been quite turned over. As has the carriage she was traveling in to attend her estranged husband's funeral. Thank heavens for Mr. Waverly, her ever dependable man of business. She shouldn't know where she'd be without him…

Lord Love a Lady Series

Nobody's Lady

(*Lord Love a Lady Series, Book 1*)

Dukes don't need help, or do they?

Michael Redmond, the Duke of Cortland, needs to be in London—most expeditiously—but a band of highway robbers have thwarted his plans. Purse-pinched, coachless, and mired in mud, he stumbles on Lilly Beauchamp, the woman who betrayed him years ago.

Ladies can't be heroes, or can they?

Michael was her first love, her first lover, but he abandoned her when she needed him most. She'd trusted him, and then he failed to meet with her father as promised. A widowed stepmother now, Lilly loves her country and will do her part for the Good of England—even if that means aiding this hobbled and pathetic duke.

They lost their chance at love, or did they?

A betrothal, a scandal, and a kidnapping stand between them now. Can honor emerge from the ashes of their love?

A Lady's Prerogative

(*Lord Love a Lady Series, Book 2*)

It's not fair.

Titled rakes can practically get away with murder, but one tiny little misstep and a debutante is sent away to the country. Which is where Lady Natalie Spencer is stuck after jilting her betrothed.

Frustrated with her banishment, she's finished being a good girl and ready to be a little naughty. Luckily she has brothers, one of whom has brought home his delightfully gorgeous friend.

After recently inheriting an earldom, Garrett Castleton is determined to turn over a new leaf and shed the roguish lifestyle he adopted years ago. His friend's sister, no matter how enticing, is out-of-bounds. He has a run-down estate to manage and tenants to save from destitution.

Can love find a compromise between the two, or will their stubbornness get them into even more trouble?

A betrothal, a scandal, and a kidnapping stand between them now. Can honor emerge from the ashes of their love?

Lady Saves the Duke

(*Lord Love a Lady Series, Book 3*)

He thinks he's saving her, but will this Lady Save the Duke, instead?

Miss Abigail Wright, disillusioned spinster, hides her secret pain behind encouraging smiles and optimistic laughter. Self-pity, she believes, is for the truly wretched. So when her mother insists she attend a house party —uninvited—she determines to simply make the best of it…until an unfortunate wardrobe malfunction.

Alex Cross, the "Duke of Ice," has more than earned the nickname given him by the ton. He's given up on happiness but will not reject sensual pleasure. After all, a man has needs. The week ought to have been pleasantly uneventful for both of them, with nature walks, parlor games, and afternoon teas on the terrace…but for some inferior stitchery on poor Abigail's bodice.

And now the duke is faced with a choice. Should he make this mouse a respectable offer and then abandon her to his country estate? She's rather pathetic and harmless, really. Oughtn't to upset his life whatsoever.

His heart, however, is another matter…

Lady at Last

(Lord Love a Lady Series, Book 4)

She can't make a baby without a husband!

Or can she?

After witnessing the miracle of birth, self-determined spinster Miss Penelope Crone is having second thoughts about swearing off marriage. She wants – no, she needs – to experience the blessed event herself. Dear God, she's practically thirty! Time is running out!

Hugh Chesterton, Viscount Danbury, is relatively intelligent, good looking, unmarried, and most importantly, close at hand. With a little décolletage, a sway of the hips, and a few drinks of brandy, Penelope is certain she can extract a respectable offer.

If only she'd accounted for the power of passion.

Because unchecked lust takes over, leaving Penelope in a most precarious predicament. And Lord Danbury –– the goose-brained jackanapes –– is proving far less attainable than she'd imagined.

Is Penelope to be cast out of society or will Lord Danbury take a leap of faith and save her from ruin? He'd better act fast if he's going to make her his lady. HIs Lady At Last...

For more info on Annabelle's Books, go to

AnnabelleAnders.com